R.W.

Délon City
Book Two of The Oz Chronicles

Single 'R' Imprint
Middlebury House Publishing,
Printed in USA

Délon City

DEDICATION:

As always For Mom, Dad, and Marianna

ACKNOWLEDGEMENTS:

No one writes in a vacuum. I truly appreciate the support and input from all my friends, family, the good people of Tullahoma, TN, and the fans of Book One. I hope Book Two lives up to your expectations.

R.W. Ridley

Délon City
Book Two of The Oz Chronicles

PROLOGUE

The man in the white coat thinks I'm crazy. Then again he's paid to think I'm crazy. He asks me for the millionth time if I've taken my medication. I ignore the question because I haven't. It's none of his business. I didn't ask to be here.

He chews on the end of a Bic pen. His black-rimmed glasses have slipped down to the end of his nose. His brown eyes peer down at me. He asks me if I want to get better. Better than what, I wonder.

The man in the white coat tries to look indifferent about my indifference, but he is frustrated. Indifferent people don't chew on the end of Bic pens. His mind is racing. He's trying to trick me into talking. He wants me to reveal myself. Get inside my head. I can't let him. I don't know who he is. I know who he says he is, but nothing is as it seems anymore.

I am the last one. Only I know where the Storytellers are.

"The Takers," he grunts. "Tell me about them again."

I look at him.

"That's right," he says. "I'm not supposed to say their name, am I?"

I smile. He knows he can say their name. Their queen is dead. I killed her. He's heard that story. He's trying to get me to talk.

"Wait, I remember now. You took out the leader. Yes, yes... how did you do that again?"

He's a bad actor.

I'm looking at him. This makes him uncomfortable. He shifts in his chair. He clears his throat. "These Takers... they ate people?"

He shifts again.

"They ate your parents? The whole town..." He flips through a notebook on his desk. "No, no, not just the town, was it... It was..."

I can't take his senseless rambling anymore. "The end," I say, "of the world."

He seems almost startled by the sound of my voice. "The end," he says hiding a smile. "That's right. I remember now, and you brought everybody back. You're a hero, Oz."

This makes me angry, and he knows it. He's pushing me. "I'm not a hero."

"Really?" He's back to chewing the end of his Bic. "You saved the world. You killed the Taker Queen. You saved the baby... what was his name?"

Nate is his name, but I won't tell the man in the white coat. I look at my hands. They are not my hands. They are too old to be my hands. I try to rub the hair off my knuckles.

"Stop that," the man shouts. "You rubbed the skin off last time."

I continue to rub.

"This is why we have to put you in restraints."

This catches my attention. I hate the restraints. I stop.

There is a moment of silence, but just a moment. The man in the white coat speaks. "Tell me why you do that."

I don't answer.

"Why do you do that to your hands, Oz?"

I laugh. "They're not my hands."

Délon City

"What do you mean?"

I hold them up and show the man in the white coat. "I'm thirteen. I can't have hands like this."

He gives me a baffled look. "What year is this, Oz?"

This is the strangest question he has asked me. "I'm not a calendar."

He picks up his small desk calendar and throws it to me.

I don't look at it.

"What year is it, Oz?"

I look down. 2033. The man in the white coat has a smug expression on his face. I throw the calendar back to him. "It's a fake."

"Look at your hands," he says. "Do those look like the hands of a 13-year-old boy?"

"Shut up!" I stand. "My name is Oz Griffin. I live in Tullahoma, Tennessee. I'm a warrior..." I pound the palm of my hand against my forehead. "We all are..."

"We?"

"Don't pretend like you don't know." I grit my teeth. "What have you done with the others?"

The man in the white coat looks through his notebook again. "You mean Wes and Lou..."

"Where are they?"

"According to you the... Délons killed them."

I collapse in the chair. "The Délons." I shut my eyes. I remember now. My mother... My bedroom... I killed the Taker Queen, and the Délons took over. But... how am I here? This is not where I am supposed to be.

The man in the white coat clears his throat again. "Perhaps that's enough for today."

With my eyes still closed I say, "Send me back." I hear the door behind me open. I turn and see a large man dressed in a ridiculously bright white uniform enter the room. His acne-scarred face is pulled taught as he flashes a phony reassuring grin.

"Chester will escort you back to your room."

I repeat my demand. "Send me back."

"As I said, Chester will escort you back..."

"Not to my room," I scream. "Send me back!"

The man in the white coat hesitates. He stands and motions to Chester to leave the room. "Oz, I want you to listen to me." He moves around the desk and stands in front of me. "There is no way back."

I hold my temper. "You know that's not true."

"It's all gone. There's nothing to go back to."

"The past is never gone," I say. "It's always there."

"What makes you think I can send you back?" he asks.

"You've done it before." I motion towards the couch in his room.

A moment of clarity washes over his face. "Hypnosis." He folds his arms over his chest and sighs heavily. "That didn't go well last time."

"I have to get back there." I am pleading now. I don't like the sound of it, but I am desperate.

"It's not real, Oz. You know that, right?"

If I tell him the truth, that he's not real. That this room we're sitting in resides only in fantasy. That the truth is in my head, back in my bedroom at home, he will never agree to send me back. "I know," I say. "But it helps me think clearly when you put me under."

He gives the matter some thought. "All right, but don't get your hopes up."

I jump up and run to the couch. "Yes, sir."

"You may be a little too wound up for it to work. You have to relax." He follows me.

Délon City

I lie down and take a deep breath.

"Relax, Oz. Just relax..." He turns down the lights. By the time he says relax again I am already slipping into a deep sleep. I have to get back.

I hear him say, "I want you to tell me what's happening, Oz. Not as if you're there, but as if it's a memory. It's very important to keep your distance."

I breathe deeply.

"A memory, Oz. That's all it is."

My eyelids are like lead.

"It's in the past."

His voice sounds farther away.

"You're on the couch in my office. You are simply telling me a story from your childhood."

Farther away.

"Do you understand?"

I think I nod in agreement, but I can't be sure.

"Where does your story begin?"

I smile. "My bedroom."

ONE

Isurvived the end of the world only to see it end again. At least that's the way it felt. I heard the words jump from my mother's lips. They cut as deep as any knife. Part of me believes she knew it, too. That she enjoyed seeing me sit dumbstruck, paralyzed by fear. I think she smiled. She lingered in the doorway of my bedroom, breathing in my despair. I sat on my bed, hopeless. The fight in me was gone.

After my Mom left my room, I rifled through my memory banks. Just a few minutes before, the world was done. It was gone. Deserted, except for a band of survivors made up of my dog, a handful of kids, a middle-aged mechanic, a talking gorilla, a shrink, and one of the greatest linebackers to ever play the game of professional football. We all fought side-by-side against a race of slobbering, greasy beasts called the Takers that consumed the entire population of the planet one-by-one. They swallowed everybody whole and transported them to some charred universe ruled over by their queen, a bigger, greasier version of the drones that had eaten the planet. And, I killed her... or it... or whatever you want to call it. It was dead. And now? Now I was here, in my bedroom, turning my Mom's words over words in my head, "Délon City."

The Délons were purple-skinned dead-eyed freaks with spider legs growing out of their heads and razor sharp mandibles that shot out of their mouths which they used to obliterate the brains of their victims. They were fierce, cold, and calculating. They turned humans into their kind. I had witnessed the transformation on the artificial turf of the Georgia Dome in Atlanta. I watched like a whimpering baby as one of my warriors, a kid not much older than me, was betrayed by my cowardice. The Délons made him one of their own.

I moved to the window of my bedroom and peered outside. The sky was an intense shade of violet. That told me everything I needed to know. I wasn't back home. Not the home I knew. The Délons ruled this world. The fight wasn't over. We had defeated the Takers only to be left with another enemy to battle, but now there was no we. It was just me.

Kimball! If I could just see his canine mug, I would feel better. I would know that I wasn't alone; that all hope was not lost.

I burst through my bedroom door. "Kimball, come here, boy!"

Nothing.

"Kimball!"

My Mom stepped out of the kitchen, a perplexed look on her thin pale face. "What are you doing, Oz? I thought I told you to get ready for school."

"I am... I mean I will. I just... I want to see Kimball."

Her confusion intensified. "Kimball, honey?"

"Yeah, Kimball. Where is he?" I was searching all of his favorite hiding places in our living room.

She walked over to me and gently placed the back of her hand on my forehead to see if I had a temperature. "Maybe you are sick, sweetie."

"What are you talking about? Where's Kimball?" I knocked her hand away. It was done out of reflex not disrespect. I had just been through a war. I wasn't in the mood to be babied.

"Oz, you know very well where Kimball is. He's gone, and

there's nothing we can do about it. I don't want to hear that name in this house again." She wasn't angry. She was sad, sadder than I had ever seen her.

"Gone?" I backed away in a daze. "What do you mean, gone?"

"Enough!" she yelled.

"Sharon." Pop's voice carried from the other room. Seconds later he appeared half-dressed for work. His pants open. His work boots untied, and his shirt unbuttoned, exposing an unimpressive chest and potbelly. "What is all the yelling about?"

"Your son refuses to obey his mother," Mom said.

"Is that right, Oz?" Pop asked.

"I just want to know where Kimball is."

Mom and Pop shared a glance. Pop cleared his throat and approached me. "I thought you understood, Oz."

"Understood what?"

"We didn't have a choice."

"I don't know what you're talking about," I said. I spotted a flaky purple rash on Pop's neck. He unconsciously scratched it with black fingernails as he spoke.

"We had to put him down, son."

The words hit me like a fist to the throat. I found myself not being able to swallow. My eyes burned from holding back the tears. I wanted to punch my father for even thinking such a thing. Kimball was a part of the family. He was a warrior. A tear escaped, and I quickly wiped it away.

Pop put his hand on my shoulder. His touch chilled me. I could see the purple rash was on his wrist, too. "It was the law, Oz. We had to."

I couldn't speak. Mom and Pop seemed to struggle with what to say as well. I could see the guilt on their faces, but I could also see the futility. They didn't want to kill my dog, but they had to. I ran to my room and slammed the door behind me.

I paced. All hope was gone. I couldn't start over again without Kimball. He was truly fearless. I was a coward pretending to be brave. I was beginning to doubt my own recollection of the events of the past few days. Maybe I didn't fight as gallantly as I remembered. Maybe I had been the recipient of dumb luck. Maybe I survived because of circumstance and not skill. I had fooled myself into believing I was a leader, but I was nothing more than some scrawny kid who wanted to get home.

I looked at my bed and thought about crawling back under the covers and wishing myself back to the Takers' universe. At least there I was a fighter. Or was I? I didn't know anymore.

I surveyed my room. It was... normal. My Tennessee Titans pendant hung above my bed. My autographed Titans football was in its case on my desk. My Titans screensaver zoomed across my computer screen. Everything was as it should be. It was too perfect. I ran my hand across the top of my desk. A sticky almost invisible residue stuck to my fingertips. That wasn't right. My Mom was the cleanest woman on the planet. She kept the house spotless. With the exception of Pop's office, you couldn't find a speck of dust with a microscope. Something was definitely wrong.

I thought about Pop's purple rash and black fingernails. He was a contractor. He was prone to smashed fingers and various other injuries. He had had plenty of black thumbnails from accidentally pounding his thumbs with a hammer at work, but I had never seen all his fingernails turn black before. And the rash? I didn't want to think what I thought, but I couldn't help it. It was almost like he was turning into a Délon .

Suddenly, I wanted out of the house. I showered and dressed as quickly as I could. My heart was pounding the whole time. I rushed to the back door to make my escape, but Mom called out just as I was stepping outside.

"Don't forget your cocoon, Oz."

I stopped and looked back. My what?

She rounded the corner carrying a red, basketball-sized, pulsating blob that emitted a katydid-like chirping. "Your Pop picked it up after change therapy last night," she said with a strange sense of pride.

I didn't know how to react. "Change therapy?"

"It just came out of the incubation center a couple of days ago." She reached behind the door and pulled my backpack off a hook.

"But..."

"I know. I know. It's a little scary, but we got a notice last week that we weren't complying fast enough with the general's transformation orders." She gently stuffed the cocoon in the backpack. "Turn around." I did as she asked and she slipped the backpack on me. I could feel the cocoon gesticulating between my shoulder blades.

"It may take two or three days, but it should hatch soon. You need to keep it close by." She kissed me on the cheek. "I'm hoping mine will hatch today." She looked at the darkest corner of the room. A bigger cocoon expanded and contracted. It emitted the same katydid chirping. "Poor thing's just too scared to come out."

I was dumfounded. I had no idea what was in the cocoons, and I had no desire to find out. I was sickened that my Mom was so excited about having the disgusting blobs in the house.

"Oh, goodness, where's my head today?" Mom said. "I almost forgot." She sped back toward the kitchen and quickly reappeared carrying a small brown paper bag. "Your father's transformation therapist suggested you eat some of these today at lunch. He said it will help your system prepare for the change. You might as

Délon City

well have a couple for breakfast since you didn't get a chance to eat this morning."

I reluctantly looked inside. Eight fat, juicy white insect larvae slowly wriggled inside the lunch bag. I gulped and nearly passed out from disgust. "You've got to be kidding me," I muttered.

"Oz, please," Mom said. "Don't be such a baby." She reached inside the bag and pulled one of the larva out. "They're not that bad." She popped the plump worm in her mouth and bit down. The ugly little maggot screamed. It actually screamed. Mom chewed it quickly and swallowed. "They don't taste that bad, and once you get used to the screaming, you're home free."

I held the bag of maggots in my hand and stared at my mother while a big chirping cocoon squirmed in the backpack I was wearing. I definitely wasn't home. The woman standing in front of me with larva remains on the corners of her mouth was most certainly not my mother, and the guy inside with a purple flaky rash and black fingernails was not my father.

I slowly descended the steps backwards, keeping a disbelieving eye on my mother as I went. Once I reached the ground I turned to run as fast and as far away as I could, but my Pop's voice rang out.

"Oz, hold up!" He kissed my mom and bounded down the steps. "I'll give you a ride."

"That's okay..."

"It wasn't a question, son. It was a statement. Learn the difference." That at least sounded like something my Pop would say.

"Yes, sir," I said. I stood and watched as the man who may or may not have been my father walked by.

He was baffled when I didn't follow him. "C'mon, get in the truck."

The truck? The truck... that meant... gas was now usable.

Cars ran. The Délons had changed that much. The Takers had somehow sabotaged the gasoline supply and rendered motorized transportation useless. The Délons returned that part of society back to normal. I could see that I was going to have to get used to a whole new set of rules.

***

The truck barreled down Lincoln Street. Pop and I had not spoken since we left the house. I was scared of the man. I stared at his head waiting for the spider legs to jet out and reach for me.

Tullahoma looked like home. But, like my bedroom, it was too normal. November was creeping up on the small little southern town, and the foliage had turned brown. The cool crisp air of the season almost sparkled it was so pure. The happy faces of the townsfolk we passed seemed to be painted on. Nothing seemed real.

My backpack with the grotesque cocoon inside it was on the seat between Pop and me. It continued to chirp.

"Annoying little booger, isn't it?" Pop said. He smiled. When he did, I could see that some of his teeth were missing. That unsettled me even more and Pop noticed. "What's wrong, boy?"

I didn't know what to say. There were so many things wrong. I didn't know how to narrow it down into one brief, coherent sentence. What could I say that wouldn't morph the man driving my Pop's truck into a full-on Délon that would devour my brains before the next traffic light?

"Nothing," I said.

"Look," he said. "Don't think I don't know this is all scary to you. Hell, it scared me, too."

"It did?"

"You bet. But it really isn't that bad. It certainly isn't like it used to be. The Délon's are more careful now."

"Careful?"

"Absolutely. They take it easy. They know transformation can be rough for us humans." He patted the backpack. "This little fella will make sure you come out of this thing okay. He's your best friend. My therapist says he comes from the best breeder in the country. He may even come from the General's stock."

"Really," I said trying to sound excited.

"You could sound a little more enthused than that, Oz. Having one of the General's solifipods is like having a blank check."

"Solifipod?"

"Cocoon, whatever you want to call it. The point is somebody in high places likes you." He pointed to the backpack. "That little shunter in there could be this family's ticket to the Royal Council."

Part of me wanted to ask him what a shunter was, but the other part of me wished I had never even heard the word. It sounded violent and painful. My instincts were to roll down my window and toss the backpack into the nearest ditch, but I knew Pop would throw a fit.

We turned into the Sergeant York Middle School parking lot. "Today's the first day of the rest of your life, or I should say the best of your life," Pop said. He pulled up to the curb and put the truck in park. He gave me a creepy half-toothed grin. "Today you get marked."

"Marked?" I didn't like the sound of it.

"I'm not going to lie to you, son. It's going to hurt. A lot." He opened his door and climbed out of the truck. "But it's worth the pain, trust me."

That was it. I had had enough quality time with freaky-turning purple-Pop. I opened my door and stepped onto the pavement with the intentions of bolting for the woods in the back of the school. But I only managed a half step before I ran into a seemingly immovable object and fell ass-first to the ground. I hit the pavement with a thud and looked up. There hovering over me was Coach Denton. I should say half of the thing standing over me was Coach Denton. The other half was a Délon with one dead eye and half its head outlined with flailing spider leg tentacles. The other eye was blue and the human half of the head was covered with a drooping comb over. The body was an impossible combination of sleek Délon design and the Coach's doughboy build. Mandibles shot out of its mouth and snapped towards me.

"Going somewhere, Oz?" the Coach hissed.

Pop came around the truck. "They always try to run on their day of marking."

Coach reached down and yanked me to my feet with his Délon hand. "Day of marking?" His dead eye bulged. "Well, congratulations, Oz." He pulled me close. "It's going to hurt like hell, but it will make a man out of you or, should I say, a Délon out of you." He cackled or hacked some disturbing sound that rattled my bones. It made me regret killing the Taker Queen.

Pop reached in the truck and pulled out my backpack. "We brought his solifipod. It should be a couple of days before his shunter comes out, but we thought it best he keep it close by."

Coach Denton sniffed the air. He held my arm tightly, and moved in closer to the backpack, breathing in deeply. "This is the general's line."

My Pop almost burst with excitement. "Really? We had been told that it was possible, but... Are you sure?"

Coach Denton breathed in even deeper. "Definitely. I've met General Roy on several occasions. This is his scent. I'd know it anywhere."

General Roy? Was it possible? Was it the Roy I knew? The warrior I had betrayed? The one I had let fall victim to the Délons?

The Coach scanned me with his dead eye. "This can only

mean one thing. You are to sit on the general's Royal Council."
He looked at my Pop. "We are not prepared for this kind of
marking."

Pop's posture visibly sank. He had never been more
disappointed. "But we got a letter. This is Oz's day of marking."
He pulled an envelope out of his back pocket and handed it to
Coach Denton.

The half-freak/half comb-over disaster let me go and read
the letter with great interest. "But I don't understand. The Minister
of Regents must be present for such a marking."

"He couldn't make it," a voice boomed. Three Délons
approached on horses from the West. They galloped across the
schoolyard. I immediately recognized the middle horse, Mr. Mobley.
Roy's horse.

Coach Denton and Pop collapsed to their knees.

The Délon who was once my friend and fellow warrior, Roy,
dismounted Mr. Mobley. "I hope I will do."

"General..." Coach Denton's voice was quivering.

Pop tried to pull me to my knees but I shook him off.

General Roy was a commanding figure. The spider legs on
his head did not flail like I had seen them do on every other Délon.
They hugged his head as if they were hairs in a tightly woven
pattern of cornrows. His milky eyes beamed confidence. He
smiled and nodded. "Oz."

"Roy," I said. Pop and Coach Denton gasped at my insolence.

The other two Délons jumped off their horses. I don't know
how, but I could tell right away they were Miles and Devlin, two
more of my former warriors.

Miles tilted his head. "Ozzie boy, how's it hanging?"

"General, this is such an honor," Pop said.

I looked at him and was disgusted by his groveling.

"The honor is mine, Mr. Griffin," General Roy said. "Your

son is a hero."

Coach Denton giggled. "Oz, a hero?"

Devlin stepped forward and slapped the Coach. "Shut up, you filthy halfer."

Pop swallowed hard. "I don't understand."

General Roy circled me as he spoke. "The legend of the Battle of Atlanta. The boy warrior. The Taker slayer. Surely you know your history, Mr. Griffin."

"Yes, sir," Pop said. "But... You mean..."

"I do indeed." General Roy knelt before me. "Meet your new king."

TWO

I sat in the principal's office alone for a long time. King? Me? It was a laughable concept. Had I not just lived through the end of the world, I would have thought this whole turn of events was a bizarre dream.

I placed my hand on the principal's desk and felt the same sticky substance that had been on my desk at home. I examined the rest of the room more closely. The walls, the filing cabinet, the clock, everything was covered in it. Even the chair I was sitting in. In fact, the substance seemed to be creeping up on my jeans and slowly covering me. I stood and wiped off as much of the goo as possible.

Roy entered, not the Roy I once knew and fought side-by-side with, but General Roy, the leader of a purple army of monstrosities that had no business ruling the planet. And I was supposed to be their king? It was too twisted to even think about.

General Roy approached me and placed his hand on my shoulder. I got the same chilling sensation that I'd had when Pop put his hand on my shoulder earlier that morning. "Oz, my friend, it is so good to see you."

I didn't feel the same, but I didn't have the guts to say it. I simply nodded.

"I know this is a lot to take in, and I wish I could give you some time to digest this new revelation, but time is something we don't have."

"What do you mean?"

He smiled. Délon smiles are not something to long for. They are wicked moments in time that are so visually disturbing they send little pricks of pain through the back of your head. "It will all be explained to you after your marking."

There was that word again, marking. I was getting tired of hearing it. It didn't exactly conjure up pleasant prospects.

Roy moved around the principal's desk and sat in the ergonomic chair. "Unfortunately, the royal scarab has not emerged yet."

"Scarab?" I couldn't recall where but I had heard that word before. I repeated the word in my mind over and over again hoping it would spark a memory.

"They are skittish little things. A nuisance really, but we can't have a marking without them. The royal scarab is particularly nasty. Has a mind of its own really."

"I don't understand..."

"Of course you don't," General Roy said. "You're still human."

"And I want to stay that way." I said expecting a fierce rebuke. But Roy simply gave me a bigger, more disturbing Délon smile.

"You only think that because you're human. Believe me, once you begin the transformation you will pray for Délon blood and Délon blood alone to run through your veins."

"Why..." I stopped myself. I was about to ask a question I didn't want to know the answer to, but Roy read my mind.

"You're wondering why I don't do it myself. Why I don't just grab you the way I was grabbed in the Georgia Dome and dig my mandibles through your skull and into your brain? Suck out your weak and feeble human essence and replace it with the glorious Délon essence?"

"Well," I said. "I wouldn't have put it that way, but, yeah."

Délon City

He laughed the same laugh I had heard on the banks of Alltoona Lake. It wasn't just him. It was a demented chorus of laughter. Every Délon on the planet was laughing through him. "A king with a sense of humor. It is just what we need." He stood and moved around the desk. "We discovered that sort of transformation is successful only during battle. We've tried it on various humans since the end of the war, but they either died or became halfers."

"Halfers? Like Coach Denton?"

He nodded. "Foul, disgusting creatures really. They're not to be trusted by either Délon or human."

The Délon version of Devlin entered the room carrying my backpack and the brown paper bag full of maggots. "Here are his things, General." He smiled and held up the paper bag. "Seven perfectly good screamers going to waste." He looked at me. "Do you mind?"

I shrugged my shoulders. "Be my guest."

Devlin reached in the bag and pulled out one of the white wriggling worms. His mandibles shot out from his mouth and snatched the maggot from his hand. The slimy little worm screamed as the mandibles retracted inside Devlin's mouth. He swallowed and sighed in pure joy. "The screaming's the best part."

I cringed.

Devlin shook his head. "I don't get humans. You don't know what's good."

Without thinking, I snickered.

"What?" Devlin was visibly upset at my unintentional laughter.

"If I remember correctly, you were human yourself not too long ago."

This set Devlin off. He charged me and grabbed me by the throat. He definitely wasn't the same Devlin I had known, the chubby little middle-schooler who spent most of his time and

19

energy looking for his next chocolate bar. That Devlin was soft and almost lovable. This Devlin was brutal and reeked of evil. "I was never human," he growled.

General Roy stood. The spider legs on his head flared for the first time. He let out a sustained. Devlin released me and backed away. I tried to massage the pain out of my throat.

"Forgive me, General," Devlin said as if he were pleading for his life.

"You dare lay your hands on our king!" General Roy approached his frightened soldier with murderous intent.

"Wait," I said through bruised vocal cords.

General Roy backhanded Devlin sending him crashing into the filing cabinets.

"Stop!" I yelled.

General Roy turned to me. "Such insolence is only punishable by death."

"But it's Devlin." I looked at the now kneeling purple beast with spider legs floundering on his head and though I didn't see one shred of Devlin in him, he was still Devlin, and I couldn't let General Roy kill him.

"You are... too human to understand." General Roy pulled a twig from the pouch he wore on his belt. The twig sprouted long willowy legs and screeched. Upon closer review it was a praying mantis of some kind. It was a foot long and anxious to get at Devlin.

"But I am your king, and I say he deserves mercy."

General Roy turned to me with a baffled expression. "Mercy?" The concept was foreign to him. "I am ordering you not to kill him."

General Roy smiled. "A human cannot order a Délon to do anything."

"But I am your king. You said it yourself."

Délon City

"You are once you are a Délon. For now, you are merely a human who is to be our king."

The praying mantis reached for Devlin, and Devlin cowered. The stick bug struggled violently to release itself from General Roy's grip.

"If I am merely human, then Devlin was not insolent for what he did."

This caused the general to pause. I could see the gears turning in his grotesque head. It was a logical argument that he could not get around. He looked at Devlin and then back at me. There was a bloodlust boiling inside him that he was fighting to control. He raised the hand that grasped the praying mantis and with a quick, forceful squeeze broke the insect in half. Breathing deeply, trying to calm himself, he stepped away from Devlin.

Devlin stood with his head down. He was in shock. He had escaped death when he fully expected to die.

General Roy was shaking. "This is mercy?"

I nodded.

"I don't like it." He spun toward Devlin. "Bring me a human."

"Yes, General," Devlin said as he bowed. He looked at me before he stepped out of the room. He clearly didn't know what to make of what just happened. I couldn't tell if he was grateful or angry.

"Why do you want a human?" I asked.

"This mercy has left a bad taste in my mouth. I must... exorcise it."

"What are you going to do?" I was panicked. Had I just spared the life of a Délon at the expense of a human?

"What I was created to do?" He scanned me from head to toe. "You are weak."

"Listen to me, you don't have to do this. The drawing. Remember the drawing? The one Hollis talked about?"

He ignored my question. "I thought you'd be stronger, but you advocate this mercy. It is for the weak." He was sounding more and more disappointed with each word.

I tried to reason with him, although clearly it was hopeless. "Hollis talked about Hyper Mental Imaging. HMI, remember? In the Georgia Dome... He said the Délons were the creation of a boy, a boy with Down syndrome who could image his visualizations onto the real world..."

"Our Storyteller, our prisoner, thanks to you."

"Thanks to me?" In an instant it was all too clear to me. Before, the Takers held the Délons' Storyteller. Because of that, the Délons were subservient to the Takers. When I killed the Taker Queen, the Délons took charge of their own Storyteller. They controlled their creator. They ruled the world because of me. I had done it again. The Takers existed because of the way I treated Stevie Dayton, and now the Délons were infesting the planet because I killed the Taker Queen.

Devlin burst through the door dragging a husky, curly-haired seventh grade boy behind him. It was Gordy Flynn. My best friend in the whole world... well, the world where Takers and Délons were nothing more than demented figments of the imagination. "Got one, boss," Devlin said grinning as he tossed Gordy toward the back wall.

"Good." General Roy reached out and gently took my face in his ice-cold hand. "We must rid you of this mercy. This one is yours."

I pulled away. "Mine?"

"Don't worry about me," he laughed. "I have my own." He pointed out the window. "You remember my... what was that word again... sister, is it?"

I turned to see another Délon standing in the school courtyard. This one had a slightly feminine air about it. It was Reya, Roy's twin sister.

"And her friend," General Roy continued.

Stepping out from behind Reya was Lou, her hands and legs in shackles, every bit as pretty and human as I had last seen her.

"Lou," I whispered.

"Yes," General Roy said. "Lou is mine." He motioned to Gordy crawling on the floor, backing into the corner of the room. "This one is yours."

"Oz," Gordy pleaded. "Help me, man."

Devlin began to cackle. "Oh, beautiful. We got us a beggar. I love it when they beg."

"What do you expect me to do?" I asked.

"Kill him," General Roy said flatly. He motioned to Reya to join us. She grabbed the chain of Lou's shackles and yanked her toward the front door.

"I'm not going to kill him," I said.

General Roy studied me. "Then you will kill the girl, and I will kill him." He stepped over to Gordy and picked him up by his curly locks.

"Nobody is killing anybody," I said. My voice cracked from trying to pass through my dry throat.

"You've killed before," General Roy said gripping Gordy's hair. He searched his pouch with his free hand and then groaned. "Devlin, your skinner." Devlin reached in his own pouch, pulled out a praying mantis and handed it to General Roy.

"I killed Takers. That's different."

I watched in horror as the new praying mantis stretched out its legs. Its head was flat like a razor blade and two eyes dangled on the end of fiber thin appendages.

General Roy held it up. "You've never seen a skinner work before, have you?"

I said nothing.

"It's a marvel really. It knows how to do two things, hate and skin its victims alive. Its favorite thing to hate is... care to guess?"

I gulped and tried not to look horrified for Gordy's sake. "Humans?"

"Bingo," General Roy said sounding pleased and excited. "Although, to be honest, they don't really care for Délons that much either. It's just that we introduced them to their favorite thing to skin. Another guess?"

I slowly shook my head.

"Humans again." He forcefully tilted Gordy's head back. The general methodically moved the stick bug closer to Gordy's ear. The closer he got the more excited the skinner became. It thrashed about violently, and I could see that its razor-blade-shaped head consisted of two thin layers that rapidly moved back and forth like a pair of electric shears. The general and Devlin laughed. "It prefers human skin. There's no accounting for taste, I guess. One skinner can devour a full-grown man's skin in three hours." He sized Gordy up. "I'm guessing curly here will take less than an hour."

"You can't do this," I said panicked.

"Wait, you haven't heard the best part." General Roy said still grinning that horrible Délon grin. "They keep their victims alive through their entire meal. After they've consumed that last morsel of human flesh... when the skinner is fat and bloated with human skin, it injects its victim with an egg sack, and within minutes the skinner larva eats the poor skinless human from the inside until there's nothing but bone. This process takes a little longer... two days maybe, and the vital organs are left in tact until the very end so the victim remains aware for as long as possible that he is being eaten alive."

"Stop," I yelled. Gordy had pissed in his pants. He was a sobbing mess. Before the Takers had come and changed my

Délon City

entire perception of life, Gordy was the tough one in our group. He was the leader of our little gang of four. I was his second. I couldn't blame him for his present state, but still part of me hated him for not shaking loose from General Roy's grip and socking the ugly creep in the mouth. That's what leaders do after all.

"Orders again, Oz?" General Roy said. "Have you already forgotten, humans cannot give Délons orders..."

"Can it, you ugly purple pile of puss!" I meant to say that in my head, but somehow it escaped my lips. Something told me saying "I'm sorry" wasn't going to get me out of trouble. My only choice was to continue with the tough guy act and hopefully buy some time until... I didn't know what I was buying time for exactly, but I was hoping it would come to me.

Fortunately or unfortunately, it worked. General Roy released Gordy and approached me with the skinner in his hand. "What did you say?" He was beyond angry. The spider legs dancing on his head told me he was quickly losing control.

"I said 'can it.'" It took every bit of my being to sound self-assured and in charge. "Stop it. Put a cork in it. Shut up. I don't want to hear any more."

General Roy grabbed me by my shirt collar and jerked me towards him until we touched chest to chest and his dead eyes were staring down at me. I could hear the scissors-like jaws of the skinner moving back and forth in his other hand. "You are testing my patience."

"And you're testing mine." I said it, but I was quickly losing my ability to sound like I meant it.

General Roy sniffed the air. "I smell fear."

"Trust me," I said. "You don't smell that great either."

His eyes narrowed. "But I smell anger, too. Maybe you aren't so weak."

The door opened and Reya stepped inside dragging Lou

25

behind her. "I'm tired of dragging this one around," Reya said. "She is skinner food, and not worthy of my time."

"Oz," Lou said.

At the sound of her voice, I suddenly found the hope I was looking for. Her expression was noble and defiant. Her will was not broken. If anything, it was stronger.

General Roy sensed a change in my manner. He pulled me even closer. His spider leg appendages danced across my head and face. "This one gives you strength." A chill ran up my spine as the tiny hairs of his spider legs moved across my skin. "Why?"

I didn't answer. Not out of defiance, but out of ignorance. Nothing else mattered now that Lou was in the room. I didn't know why. I just knew I would do anything to keep her safe.

"She might be useful." The general released me. "But this one is useless." He motioned to Gordy, and then held out the skinner. "Kill him."

I swallowed hard and surveyed the room. The skinner's jaws were moving faster now. It sensed it was about to eat.

"The skinner feeds on the fearful and obeys the fearless," General Roy said. "Which are you?"

There was only one thing to do. I took a deep breath and let it out. Before one more shred of doubt entered my mind, I took the skinner from the general and held it at arm's length. It squirmed and hissed and turned its eyes toward me. I told myself to be fearless, to control the flesh-eating bug as it contemplated whether I was food or master. I told myself this, but I had no idea if it would work. Much to my surprise and joy, the skinner's eyes turned back toward Gordy. I sighed in relief, and then felt a wave of confusion as I realized that I was happy the bug wanted to eat my best friend instead of me. I still needed to find a way out of killing Gordy.

"C'mon, Oz," Gordy said. "It's me, man, Gordy."

Délon City

I stepped toward him. My brain cramped from racing so fast. I needed a plan, and I needed it fast. Another step. There was no way I could kill Gordy, but I knew if I didn't, General Roy would use Lou as leverage. I couldn't let anything happen to her. The skinner lashed out and almost leapt from my grip. Another step. General Roy watched me with anticipation. He was hungry to watch Gordy die, to watch anyone die. He was almost drooling. Lou shook her head. Her eyes begged me not to do it. Reya cackled and Devlin was jittery with joy. The room felt as if it was about to implode from the tension.

"Do it!" Reya screamed.

"This is beautiful," Devlin giggled.

Another step, and I still had no plan. It was looking more and more like I was about to lose my best friend... again. Another step. One more and I couldn't stall any longer. The last step. I knelt down. Gordy closed his eyes tight. The skinner whipped about violently. It was about to feed. There was only one thing left to do. As if my arm was moving through molasses, I extended it toward Gordy, all the time praying for a way out of killing my best friend.

THREE

Délon Miles burst through the door. "The royal scarab has emerged." His voice was full of excitement.

General Roy grabbed my arm. "No time for fun," he said, snarling with disappointment. He took the skinner from me and stuck it in his pouch. "The royal scarab awaits."

Gordy fainted. He had been saved by the bell, or in this case the scarab. I was happy for him, but I also knew that the emergence of the royal scarab meant I was about to undergo something called a marking. All I knew about this much anticipated procedure is that it was painful, very painful.

I was yanked to my feet by Miles and Devlin and escorted to the door. Lou and I shared a quick glance. She looked different. I couldn't put my finger on it, but there was something about her that wasn't the same. She smiled, and I was immediately filled with courage.

Devlin and Miles continued to drag me down the hallway. General Roy led the way. He walked with purpose. It was apparent this marking meant a lot to him.

We reached the nurse's office, and the general threw open the door. Devlin and Miles tossed me inside.

"The lights," General Roy said.

Devlin picked up a nearby mop, and Miles grabbed a broom. They started smashing the florescent lights overhead.

I ducked my head and backed away. "You guys ever hear of a light switch?"

Délon City

Once all the lights were broken, Pop entered the room carrying a box covered with a black cloth. "This is such an honor, son." He placed the box on the examination table.

General Roy approached. "This is a day Délons will celebrate until the end of time."

"You want to clue me in here?" I said. "What am I supposed to do?"

The general removed the black cloth from the box revealing an aquarium. A round beetle about the size of a fist with a scorpion's tail scampered about the glass enclosure.

"You don't have to do anything," General Roy said. "The royal scarab will do all the work."

I suddenly remembered what scarab meant, beetle. The skinners, the screamers, the scarabs, the spider legs on the head, the insect mandibles in the mouths, I was beginning to see a theme here. This Storyteller had a thing for bugs. I hated bugs.

General Roy ordered all the others out of the room. He turned to me. "I wish I could stay for this, but the marking is a solitary event."

"In that case, take the beetle-thingy with you," I said.

He cocked his head and thought about my request. After a few moments of pondering he laughed. "Another joke. I get it." He backed out of the room and closed the door.

The room was dark, but I could still see. Escaping through the only door was useless. The general and the others would be waiting for me. There was a small window that was sealed shut. The second I broke the glass they would be on top of me. My only recourse was to kill the beetle..., which was gone.

In my haste to formulate an escape plan, I had taken my eye off the royal scarab. Big mistake. I heard a humming above my head. It zipped and soared. The fist-sized beetle had wings. It blended in with the dark background so I couldn't see it, but I could hear it flying back and forth. It was looking for me, no doubt.

I picked up a metal tray on the nearby counter. The beetle buzzed by my ear, and I swung the tray blindly. The other ear. I jumped back and continued to swing the tray, missing my target with every swat. In my big book of fun, swatting at a sadistic scorpion beetle with a metal tray in the dark while it buzzed my head didn't make the list.

It hit me with a thud on the arm, and I screamed like a little baby. My adrenaline was through the roof. I swung the tray like I was the homerun king. In a moment of complete panic and sheer luck, I heard a heavy whack as I whirled the tray forward. I hit it. A clunk shortly followed, and I knew it was on the floor somewhere in front of me. Instinct told me I hadn't killed it, merely knocked it out of commission briefly. Time was of the essence. I knelt down with the tray raised above my head. I was going to kill it and be done with this whole marking thing before it started.

I frantically searched the floor in front of me. Nothing. I bent down, slowly, carefully, my eyes peeled for the bug. The skin on my right arm crawled. My whole body was tied up in knots. I felt a twinge in my gut. The anticipation was excruciating. The skin on my right arm crawled again... Only it wasn't my skin crawling. It was something crawling on my right arm. Attached to my forearm with thousands of tiny little hooks at the end of its six little legs was the royal scarab. I stared at it motionless. If this had been the old west, this would have been the stare down in a gunfight, each gunslinger waiting for the other to make a move. Who would be first out of the holster? I flinched first. Another big mistake. The beetle's pinchers sank into my skin. I felt a searing pain followed by a complete relaxation of my right arm. My arm flopped to the floor. I could feel it, but I couldn't move it. The rest of my body soon followed. I lay on my back, unable to move, but still able to feel all my extremities. In fact, there was a heightened sense of feeling in my body. It was as if every nerve ending was pumped full of some kind of happy juice that made me extra aware of every inch of my skin all at once. It was maddening.

I felt the royal scarab march up my arm. I felt its little prickly feet dig into my skin as it made its way onto my shoulder and then my face. I tried to blow it off, but I couldn't muster up even the slightest little puff. I wasn't even sure if I was breathing at all.

The beetle paused at my nose and probed inside my nostrils with its pinchers, never biting me, just toying with me. I could see the dark hump of its back. It moved past my nose and inched toward my left eye, its tiny feet digging into me deeper and deeper all the way. Inside my head, I could hear its mandibles rubbing together.

Its beetle eyes looked into my left eye. It let out a deafening screech, and then in a quick almost indiscernible motion it extended its scorpion tail and stung me in the corner of my left eye.

The pain was unbearable. It was as if the eye was plucked from the socket. My whole head felt as if it were on fire and inflated to twice its normal size. I just knew it was going to pop at any moment. I wanted to pass out. I wanted to go to sleep and never wake up again, but I couldn't.

A flood of light entered the room as the door opened. General Roy hovered above me, smiling that hideous Délon smile.

***

My eye burned and throbbed for hours after the marking. I'm sure the venom from the royal scarab bite that had heightened all my senses heightened my sense of pain, too. The pain in turn brought with it a hyper sense of anger. I was mad as hell. At everything and nothing in particular. I wanted to tear the world apart. My heart pumped lava through my veins. Steam was coming out of my ears. I thought about the skinner in my hand earlier. It twitched and squirmed anxious to get at Gordy, and I held it back. Why did I hold it back? Why didn't I let it kill Gordy? Lying there with my eye swollen shut, I couldn't make sense of my desire to save Gordy's life. It seemed unnatural.

I was back in my bedroom. I don't exactly remember how I ended up there. I was aware of nothing but my own body and thoughts and senses. As the pain subsided, bits and pieces of the previous hours came back to me. General Roy and the others had escorted my father's truck back home. I lay in the bed of the truck barely alive. They were all rejoicing in my pain and misery. They knew it was bringing me one step closer to being one of them.

Nightfall was upon Tullahoma when I was able to sit up in my bed without wanting to wretch. With my good eye, I spotted my solifipod in the corner of the room. It was expanding and contracting in slow even movements. I was surprised that I did not have the same level of disgust for it that I had had before. In fact, a small part of me was glad to see it. Pop had called it my best friend. Somehow that wasn't such a crazy notion anymore.

Intellectually, I knew the marking had done something to me, but I was starting not to care, and that scared me. It was as if there were two people living inside my head. One clinging to my past, fighting for the old world. The other, if not embracing the notion of joining the Délons, certainly not putting up much of a fight.

I sat on the edge of my bed not wanting to stand, but somehow feeling I had to. My knees gave way as soon I stood, and I fell. I placed my hand on the wood floor and attempted to push myself up. The wood plank moved underneath my hand. I examined it more closely. Digging my fingernails into the seams, I was able to remove the loose board, uncovering a small secret compartment. I reached inside and pulled out a photograph. It was the picture of Nate and his parents that I had saved for him. An exhausted Mrs. Chalmers cradled her newborn son in her arms while Mr. Chalmers proudly sat at her bedside.

I stared at the picture for what seemed an eternity. I studied every inch of it. I thought about Stevie's comic book and how, for some inexplicable reason, he had made me the hero of his story. Looking after Nate, that felt... noble. I wanted that feeling again.

I don't know how the picture got in my room in a secret compartment in the floor next to my bed, but it was obvious that I was meant to find it then, at the time when I was having thoughts of giving in to the Délons.

I stuck the photo in my back pocket, and I forced myself to my feet. I was cold. The room wasn't cold. I was cold from the inside out. My bones felt as if they were frozen and my muscles were ice crystals. The hate I had felt earlier was finding a target. If I ever got my hands on that fat little royal scarab, I was going to pluck it apart ugly little bug part by ugly little bug part.

I opened the door to my bedroom. The house was dark. Miles was lying on the couch, snoring away like he didn't have a care in the world. It was good to see him sleeping. Délons slept. They were at least that human. If they slept, that meant they had vulnerabilities. If they had vulnerabilities, that meant they could be defeated.

I backed into my room and closed the door. I was shivering uncontrollably. I felt as if I would shatter at any moment. As quietly as possible, I tore through my dresser and found the heaviest sweater I owned. After finding my favorite blue jean jacket, I opened my bedroom window and stumbled into the crisp cold world outside what was once my home.

The wind howled through the bare branches of the trees in the neighborhood. My vision limited to one eye and my movement severely impaired by frozen insides, I clumsily navigated my way to the Chalmers' house. Climbing the steps to their front porch took every effort. Knocking on their door bruised my fragile knuckles, and seeing Mrs. Chalmers when she opened the door nearly broke my heart. She was a halfer.

The brutal-looking beast sniffed the air. Her milky Délon eye zoomed back and forth while her human hand reached out and caressed my swollen left eye. "You've been marked."

"Mrs. Chalmers..."

"You shouldn't be here," she said concerned.

"I have to find Nate."

"Nate?" Her human eye brightened. "I know that name."

"Your son, Mrs. Chalmers..."

A drunken voice roared from the staircase behind her. "Who's at the door?"

She didn't answer.

"Answer me, you ugly cow!"

I peered around her and saw a Délon standing at the top of the stairs with a bottle of whisky in its hand. It was Mr. Chalmers.

"I said who is it? Speak, you stinking halfer!"

I stepped past Mrs. Chalmers and entered the house. "It's me... Mr. Chalmers." It sounded funny calling the monster at the top of the stairs Mr. Chalmers, but I didn't know what else to call him.

He stomped down three stairs trying to focus his dead eyes on me. "Me who?"

"Oz Griffin."

"Oz..." His posture changed. He dropped the whisky bottle

and barreled down the remaining stairs. "Oz Griffin. Oz Griffin."
He fell to his knees. "Forgive me, Oz Griffin."

"Forgive you?" I looked at Mrs. Chalmers. She bowed her
head in shame. "For what?"

"I know it is forbidden to keep halfers in your home, but
what am I to do, she is from my... before I transformed. Before I
was reborn Délon ." Mr. Chalmers was shaking more than me.
He was scared for his life.

Mrs. Chalmers screamed. "I am only this way because you
made me this way!"

"Shut up!" The Délon growled. His fear was quickly replaced
by intense anger. I could empathize with him. I knew that anger.
I longed for that anger when I saw it in him.

"I will not. You broke the law. You couldn't wait for my
marking. You broke the law."

Mr. Chalmers grabbed my pant leg. He began to plead. "I
only wanted her to know the beauty of being Délon . The glorious
hatred, the pure fury, the cleansing..."

"Anger?" I said.

"Yes, yes. I wanted her to feel it, to know it, to become it."

"You broke the law," Mrs. Chalmers repeated.

"It is an unjust law. You were filthy with your human essence.
I wanted it out of my house."

"You knew what it would do to me. You knew I would become
this."

Mr. Chalmers looked at me. "It's not true. I had studied the
old way. I read about the method used in battle. I performed it
on her. I thought it would work."

I backhanded the Délon kneeling before me. I did it without
thinking. It brought me a pleasure that I had never known before.
I wanted to do it again. I wanted to rip the flesh from his bones.
The wanting flushed away the coldness. I knew if I hit him again

my blood would begin to boil and it would bring me the strength of ten men. I backed away. "You broke the law."

The Délon stood, his dead eyes full of rage. "No human hand shall ever be raised against a Délon. That is the law you have broken."

Hunched over, he stepped toward me and again without thinking, I sent my fist crashing into his face. I heard his bones crack. "Do you know who I am?"

He rubbed his jaw. "I know who you will be. That does not change the law. No human shall..."

I smashed him in the face again. "I am the law." My strength was increasing with each punch. I wouldn't have been surprised if with the next punch I decapitated him.

I looked at Mrs. Chalmers and for a moment I understood the Délons' disgust for halfers. She was beyond ugly. She was an abhorrent mistake of nature. I wanted to kill her, to end her existence so I would never have to look at her again.

Mr. Chalmers was not done with me. He wobbled from the blows and the alcohol, but he was going to rush me at any moment. I could feel his need to attack. I raised my hand. "Get out of my sight before I call for the general."

The message got through to him immediately. The general would not show the restraint that I had demonstrated, and Mr. Chalmers knew it. He located his whiskey bottle and raced up the stairs.

I made an effort not to look at Mrs. Chalmers until I could calm myself. If I saw her ugly halfer face, it would have taken every bit of strength inside of me not to rip her limb from limb. I breathed in and out trying to soothe the beast within. Gradually, my insides began to freeze again. I started to shiver. I felt a hand wrap around my shoulder. I turned to see half of Mrs. Chalmers' smiling face. "You should sit down." She guided me to living room and helped me to the sofa.

"It's so cold," I said.

"They're punishing you." She placed her hand on my knee.

"Punishing me?"

"You've been marked. They're with you now. They can feel the Délon ways inside of you. When you fight them, they punish you."

"How do I make it stop?"

"You become a Délon." She said it coldly as if it were inevitable.

I reached in my back pocket and pulled out the picture. "Nate, Mrs. Chalmers." I handed it to her. "I have to find him."

She lightly moved her human fingers across the glossy surface of the photograph. I couldn't detect the slightest bit of recognition in her human eye. The spider legs on the Délon half of her head danced wildly. "Who are these people?" she asked.

"You, Mrs. Chalmers. Your family."

She looked at me. "Family?"

Hearing her say the word "family" I realized that it was more than her not recognizing the fact that she had a family. She had no idea what the concept of family was.

"Think, Mrs. Chalmers. Nate was born just a few weeks ago. Don't you remember?"

A tear formed in her human eye. "Don't make me remember, Oz Griffin." She was pleading. "Don't make me remember."

"I have to find him..."

Whispering, she said. "If you find him, they will find him." She sniffed the picture. "He is a beautiful baby." She screamed in pain. Breathing heavily she repeated, "He is a beautiful baby." Her pain intensified. She threw the picture at me. "He would make lovely skinner food." Her pain eased.

To my horror, a small part of me understood her sentiment. A horde of skinners would dispose of the fragile little body in seconds, and it would be a sight to see. A sight any Délon would enjoy. I shook the thought out of my head and stood. "This will be over soon, Mrs. Chalmers."

She didn't say a word. She stared straight ahead.

"Mrs. Chalmers?"

"I'm ashamed, Oz."

"I know..."

"I like feeling this way." The tears fell from her human eye. "Why is that?"

"Because, Mrs. Chalmers." I hesitated. "Because nothing is as it should be." I turned to leave, but stopped. Without looking back I said, "I'm going to fix this. I'm going to find Nate. I'm going to find them all, every last Storyteller, and I'm going to fix this." I don't know if she understood what I was saying, but it didn't really matter. I wasn't really talking to her. They were listening. I could feel it. Every Délon knew my every move. They heard my every word, my every thought. There was no escaping them. They were inside my head, and I was inside theirs. I wasn't going to hide from them. I was going to kill them, and I wanted them to know there was nothing they could do to stop me.

I didn't want to go home. As I stood there in the middle of the street, I could think of only one place I could go.

FOUR

Every step of the mile walk to Stevie Dayton's house felt as if millions of tiny knives were being shoved through the bottoms of my feet. I stood at the front door, trying to catch my breath, to put the pain out of my mind, to summon the courage to actually knock. My biggest fear was that Stevie would somehow answer the door. That he would stand there looking at me, making me feel intolerably guilty for the way I had treated him. Worst of all, I was afraid he would forgive me, and it would mean nothing to me because of what the marking had done.

Unable to put it off any longer, I knocked. Heavy footsteps approached. The door swung open, and Délon Reya stood there, chuckling at my stunned expression.

"What are you doing here?" I said.

"Welcome to our little home away from home." She stepped back and invited me to enter.

I thought about running, but I knew chasing me down would give them too much pleasure. They loved it when you ran. I moved past her and turned to the living room. Mrs. Dayton sat stiff and nervous on the couch next to General Roy. Lou sat on the floor chained to a large antique bookcase. Mrs. Dayton was as I remembered her, a plump woman aged beyond her forty plus years, her grayish blonde hair disheveled, her hands spotted and rough.

"Mrs. Dayton..."

"Ahhh, our conquering hero," General Roy said. "My, my, you really are a strong one, aren't you? Most humans take days before they can even sit up after their marking. You've managed to take a spin around the neighborhood after only a few short hours."

"He stinks of halfer." Reya shoved me into the room and took a seat on the other side of Mrs. Dayton.

"What is this?" I said.

"This?" General Roy smiled. "This is a party."

"Are you all right, Mrs. Dayton?" My concern for her pained me. It felt as if I were being poked in the heart with a flaming needle. I grabbed my chest.

Mrs. Dayton did not answer. She could not. She moaned and gurgled. It was horrific.

Reya laughed. "What's the matter, cat got your tongue?" She grabbed Mrs. Dayton's face and forced her to open her mouth. Her tongue had been removed.

The general stuck his finger in Mrs. Dayton's mouth and twirled it around. "I can't put my finger on it, but something's missing." He laughed at his own sick joke. He turned to me. "You see I have a sense of humor, too. We will make a good team, you and me."

Reya's expression soured. She didn't like me when she was a human. She didn't like me now. Some things never change.

"Why did you cut out her tongue?" I wanted to look away, but I couldn't.

"We didn't," Reya said. "Not our style."

"Not at all," General Roy said. "This is the work of a silencer."

"Silencer?"

"Canter is its name." The general stood. "Oh, yes, I keep forgetting. You've missed so much. Silencers, the invention of our second Storyteller."

40

My already frozen blood went even colder. "Second Storyteller?"

"Don't look so surprised. They're not that hard to find really. They are stupid, whimpering, tortured souls. They might as well wear a nametag, 'Hello my name is Donald and I'm a Storyteller.'"

"Donald?"

"Donald Freeman, a dishwasher somewhere in New Jersey. He's 57, and every day of those 57 years he was mocked, ridiculed and humiliated by poor pathetic humans. It's sad really." He laughed. "Okay, more funny than sad, but still you can't help but understand the monster he was driven to create. A silencer, a foul loathsome creature that dines on fresh human tongues. No human would ever be able to make fun of our Donald again." He wiped away a fake tear. "And since we control their Storyteller, they are quite useful as our servants. They dine on the tongues we wish them to dine on."

"Why... Mrs. Dayton?"

General Roy sat back down beside Mrs. Dayton, put his arm around her and pulled her in close. "The old bag wouldn't talk, so we decided she didn't need her tongue. I asked Canter to enjoy a snack on me." He held her chin up with his index finger.

"You pig!" My blood began to speed through my veins. The anger was building up inside of me, and with each passing second the frozen pain quickly began to disappear.

General Roy stood and approached me. "Don't fight it, Oz. The anger is good. Misguided in your case, but good, nonetheless. It's what being a Délon is all about."

"Shut up," I said. I pushed the palm of my hands to my forehead. I had to keep it together. I couldn't give them what they wanted. "Mrs. Dayton doesn't know anything..."

"She knows the Source," Reya barked. She jerked Mrs. Dayton by her arm.

"The Source? What Source?"

"The beginning," General Roy said. "She knows what it is. We must find it. We must protect it."

"The beginning?"

"Of Délons," General Roy said. He was growing increasingly impatient.

I moved towards Lou. "What makes you think she knows anything about Délons? This is where the Takers' Storyteller lived. He had nothing to do with Délons." I bent down and examined Lou's wrists. They had been rubbed raw from the shackles. "Are you all right?" I whispered.

She forced a smile and nodded.

"Relax," Reya said. "Your girlfriend is fine."

"She's not my girlfriend." It was a stupid thing to deny. It was of little importance given the current circumstances, but somehow the adolescent part of me found it necessary to clarify.

Reya stood excited. "Good, then let's kill her. My skinner needs to feed." She reached for her pouch.

I stood between Reya and Lou. "Not going to happen."

Reya stepped forward, but stopped when General Roy motioned for her to step back. She hesitated. Her spider legs danced and reached for me. She was disinclined to follow the general's orders, but she forced herself to comply and sat back down on the sofa.

"Unchain her," I said bending back down next to Lou.

"How did you put it?" General Roy said. "Not going to happen."

"Her wrists are bleeding. She'll get an infection."

"She is an infection," Reya said.

"I said unchain her."

They ignored me.

I stood and confronted General Roy. "Look, maybe you've

forgotten what it's like to be human, but we can get sick and die. If she dies, then you don't get your king."

General Roy snapped. He let out a loud roar and lifted me by the collar of my blue jean jacket. "You would do well not to remind a Délon that they were once human. It is not a thing we remember fondly." His corn rowed spider legs unfurled, one slashing me across the face. His hatred grew until I thought his head would explode. Then, almost as suddenly as his fury came, he suppressed it and dropped me to the floor. "Release her," he said to Reya.

Reya stood in a huff. "I will not."

General Roy did not take kindly to defiance. He rushed his sister without notice and ripped a spider leg from her head. "Release her, or I will pluck them all."

Reya howled in pain. Her head wound oozed a thick purple substance that slowly ran down her cheek. "Why do you let this human order you around?"

"He will be king soon enough." He shoved Reya to the floor next to Lou. "Besides she will not run. She is loyal to our friend." He put his arm around me. He seemed almost jolly, as if plucking the spider leg from Reya's head was an instant mood enhancer. "You asked a question before... oh, yes. This is not just the house of the Takers' Storyteller. This is the birth of the end. We are the end, Oz, and we must protect our Source in order to reign forever."

"Let me get this straight." I scratched my head. "You don't even know what the Source is?"

Reya finished unchaining Lou. Lou ran to Mrs. Dayton's side and comforted her.

"We do not," General Roy said. "But what creature does?"

"True, but you say Mrs. Dayton does know?" I said.

"The old hag knows," Reya barked.

"So, you cut out her tongue?" I shrugged my shoulders. "I guess it's safe to say you Délons aren't the sharpest tools in the shed."

"Meaning?" The General said.

"Meaning, if I found the one person who knows my Source, I wouldn't eliminate her main form of communication so she couldn't tell me."

General Roy snickered. He moved to the sofa and tossed Lou to the floor. He reached down and picked up Mrs. Dayton's left arm. I had not noticed it before. It was nothing more than a stump. The hand had been severed at the wrist. "That is why we did not cut off her right hand, so she can write down the information we need."

For the first time since the marking, I felt real fear. It was a blistering cold that quickly engulfed my entire body. It was nothing like the cold I felt in my muscles and bones when I fought the Délon ways that were taking root inside me. It was a burning cold, a cold that seeped deep inside my nerves and shook me until I longed for... the taste of blood. It didn't make any sense. I was afraid for my life, yet all I could think of was drinking the blood of some poor wretched... human. Somehow, I knew the warm living blood of a human would make the bitter cold go away.

General Roy looked at Reya and smiled. "His first."

Reya stepped toward me. "He feels it?"

"The craving. It is unmistakable." The general spoke as if he were a proud father.

"But it's too soon. His shunter has not..."

"Stop talking about me like I'm not here," I said. I was exhausted from fighting the cold. I placed my hands on my knees and struggled to breathe normally.

General Roy picked Lou up by her hair. "Take the King into the first bedroom down the hall."

"Let go of me," Lou screamed.

Without thinking I leapt forward and grabbed the general's

wrist. I could have broken his arm with no effort. I felt the strength in my grip and knew that the general was no match for me. From the look in his dead eyes, he knew it too. "Hands off your queen." I smiled. It was that Délon smile I had so despised just hours before, but I couldn't help it. It was a part of me now. They were a part of me.

"Queen?" Reya said. She huffed and set out to throw a tantrum, but her brother stopped her with a simple slow tilt of his head. "But I am to be queen." She looked as if she would cry.

I laughed. "Not going to happen."

"But it is by order of the Royal Council. I am to be queen." She stomped her foot. The tantrum was coming despite her brother's wishes.

"Enough, Reya," General Roy barked.

"But..."

"This is a matter for the Council."

"It is a matter that has already been decided." Her defiance was bordering on suicidal. She had to know that the general was about to explode.

"I am the king. It is my choice," I said.

"Don't I get a say in this?" Lou asked.

"Shut up, human," Reya said, her voice reaching a disturbingly high pitch. She turned her venom on me. "You are not king yet. You are merely marked. Until your shunter finishes with you, you are just another filthy human. You'd be wise to remember that."

General Roy managed to release his arm from my grip. In a shockingly tender voice he said to me, "You should let the human... Lou show you to the bedroom. You need some rest. This can all be settled later."

I wanted to settle it then. I wanted to rip Reya apart, but the superhuman strength I had felt just seconds before was gone. She would tear me to shreds. I reluctantly agreed and backed away. Lou gently took me by the arm and led me to the bedroom. I was asleep on my feet before we even made it to the hallway.

***

I woke up several hours later in Stevie Dayton's bedroom. With the sun peeking through the blinds above the bed, I felt refreshed. It was almost impossible for me to grasp, but I actually felt... good. I looked to my left and saw Lou's warm and gentle face looking back at me. I quickly went from good to great.

"The pain is gone?" she asked.

I nodded. The sound of her voice lifted my spirits even higher.

"I've heard that it is a remarkable feeling when you awake from your marking..."

"It didn't feel so good last night," I said.

"Just because you were conscious doesn't mean you were awake."

I sat up, stretching my arms, sucking in the cool air of Stevie's room. "You haven't been marked?"

She shook her head. "Haven't had the pleasure." I noted a hint of sarcasm in her voice. "Roy and Reya remember me from... before, but they're not exactly sure what to do with me. I guess they were waiting for you to show up."

"Waiting? It's only been a couple of days... if that."

She cocked her head and raised an eyebrow. "A couple of days? It's been months since you destroyed the Taker Queen."

"Months?" I studied her baffled expression. "It just happened..."

"It was almost a year ago. More maybe."

That was what was different about her. She wasn't twelve anymore. She was thirteen. She was a year older. I stood up and looked at myself in the mirror above Stevie's dresser. Had I aged a year? Was it possible the gangly kid I was staring at in the mirror was fourteen years old? "I don't get it. Mom and Pop acted like I had been there the whole time. That it was just another morning."

"It had been to them," Lou said. "It's hard to explain. Let's just say time doesn't really make much sense anymore. It kind of jumps all over the clock. Ever since the Storytellers changed everything, things have been kind of chaotic."

"Tell me about it." I examined my once swollen left eye. It was completely healed now. There was just a slight bruising where I'd been stung, but other than that, you would have never known it was swollen to the size of a grapefruit just a few hours before.

In the mirror, I could see Lou standing behind me now. I remembered seeing her that first time in Manchester. Her hair was tangled and unruly and her face was covered with dirt. She was afraid to talk because of the Takers. Wes protected her like he was her father... I turned to her in a moment of desperation. "Wes? Where is he? The others, where are they?"

She tried to remain stoic, but she couldn't. Her face sank into a morbid expression of despair. "I was hoping you could tell me." She began to sob. "I miss them so much."

I didn't know what to do. Lou was a rock. She had been emotional before, but never had I seen her so inconsolable. I moved closer to her. Hugging her seemed wrong for some reason, but I didn't know why. I reached out and patted her back. "It's going to be all right."

She practically lunged for me and buried her head in my chest. "I don't know what to do," she said. "The Délons, they're not like the Takers." She looked up at me with tearful eyes. "We can't beat them."

"We can if we find the Source before they do." I said with unfounded confidence. I made it sound as if it were the simplest solution to the most complicated problem in the world. Like we could actually do it. In reality, I agreed with her. We couldn't beat the Délons. They were smarter than the Takers. They were organized and militant. The Délons were here to build something, a world they could rule with absolute authority.

Lou did not detect the doubt in my voice. "Do you know where it is?"

I shook my head. "Well, no..."

"Do you even know what it is?"

"Not exactly, but..."

"What makes you so sure that we can find it before they do?" she asked.

I gave her a stern, unflinching look. "Because we have to."

She buried her head in my chest again. "I don't think that's enough this time."

I did what my mother used to do to me when I was a kid and couldn't stop crying. I patted her back and said, "There, there." They were the two most repeated words I heard until I decided I was too old to let my mother see me cry. "There, there." The words made me feel like... I was home, safe from the thing that had made me so upset in the first place. I tried to convey this same feeling to Lou as we stood there in Stevie Dayton's room contemplating the end of the human race. I did this until I noticed a picture on the wall. It was a drawing, a masterful drawing of a Délon-like creature. It was crouched with well-muscled legs. Its hands were gnarled and it was in an attack posture. Its mouth was open and the razor sharp mandibles were snapping in the air. Its spider legs danced on its head. Its cold dead eyes stared at me. It was a perfect rendition of a Délon. Not a Délon really. More than a Délon. There wasn't a hint of humanity in the creature in the drawing. What was it doing in Stevie's room?

I released Lou and moved towards the drawing. The startling image seemed to glare at me as I approached it. The artist had signed it on the lower right-hand corner. Clancy... something. The writing was chicken scratch. I couldn't make out the last name.

"What is it?" Lou asked. She sat on the bed.

"This drawing..." I looked around the room. The walls were covered with drawings of monsters from Stevie's imagination. They were good, but not as finely detailed as the drawing of the Délon. "Why is it here?"

Lou was unimpressed. "Stevie liked to draw."

"He didn't draw this one."

"How do you know?"

"For one thing, Stevie died before the Délons ripped a purple hole in the sky and, for another, this one is signed by a Clancy somebody." I moved in to get a closer look.

Lou stood and joined me in my sudden fascination with the picture. "Who's Clancy?"

"I don't know." The picture was amazing. The more I stared at it, the more detail I picked up. The artist had even included drawings of skinners and scorpion beetles.

The door to the bedroom opened. Mrs. Dayton stood in the hallway, hiding her mutilated left hand behind her back. Her lips pressed together, she nodded her head and walked away.

"I think we're supposed to follow her," I said.

"Yeah" Lou said. "You first." She gently pushed me ahead of her.

I reluctantly left the bedroom with Lou holding onto my arm and followed Mrs. Dayton down the hall. I didn't think Mrs. Dayton was dangerous, but she moved with a deliberateness that unsettled me.

Mrs. Dayton pushed through the swinging door that led to the kitchen. Lou and I watched as the door swung back and forth in smaller and smaller increments until it stopped.

"Well," I said. "We should go in."

"I guess," Lou answered.

"Let's go then."

"I'm right behind you."

"What do you think she wants?"

"To thank you for torturing and belittling her son until he committed suicide and in doing so causing the end of the world as we know it." She said it in one excited breath.

"Hmmmm?" I said.

"What?"

"Oh nothing. I was just remembering the good old days when you didn't talk."

The kitchen door swung open sending Lou and me into a series of ear piercing screams. Mrs. Dayton stood on the tile floor of the kitchen, shocked by our reaction. She smiled, trying to put us at ease and motioned for us to come in. With some hesitation, we entered the kitchen.

We were immediately struck by the smell of bacon and freshly baked biscuits. The kitchen table was set for three. Pancakes and seemingly every other kind of breakfast food were neatly displayed in the center of the round table. Lou and I quickly sat down. I buried my plate in hash browns, scrambled eggs, sausage, silver dollar pancakes covered in maple syrup, bacon and homemade buttery biscuits. Every bite tasted as if I were sampling each food for the first time. It was a feast fit for a... king.

Lou covered her plate with the pancakes and drowned them in a thick lake of syrup followed by a pile of powdered sugar. I got a sugar rush just looking at it.

Mrs. Dayton sat at the table and sipped a piping hot cup of black coffee. She kept her left hand hidden from view. I glanced at her while I ate. Her face was relaxed, much more relaxed than it had been the night before. General Roy and Reya were gone, and they weren't coming back. I could tell from Mrs. Dayton's expression. They were through with her for now. She had served a purpose. They had made her suffer because of me. I had done this to her. They knew she didn't know who or what the Source was. They were sending a message to me. Others would suffer in great numbers if I didn't help them. For some reason they thought I knew, and they were going to torture and mutilate others until I told them what they wanted to know. They were desperate.

Time was running out. That was what the general had alluded to at school the day before. They couldn't wait for me to finish the transition. They needed to know where the Source was ASAP. They were desperate. Which meant in a strange way, I had the upper hand.

Lou and I didn't talk during breakfast. I guess we thought it would be rude since Mrs. Dayton couldn't join the conversation. We lapped up our breakfast like it was our last meal. Our bellies full, we leaned back in our chairs and soaked in the feeling of complete satisfaction. It was a rare feeling, one I hadn't felt since... the moment I found myself in my bed after having killed the Taker Queen. The moment just before my mother said those words to me. I belched a little and asked, "Where is Délon City?"

"Where it's always been," Lou said. She was struck by a sudden dose of memory. "Oh, that's right, I forget you're not exactly caught up on the... new world. It's Atlanta."

"Atlanta? The Titans are playing the Falcons this weekend. They still play football?"

"Not exactly," Lou said. "Not the way you're thinking any way." She looked at Mrs. Dayton. Mrs. Dayton gave her an approving nod. "First of all," Lou continued, "it's not the NFL. It's something completely different. They don't play with a ball." She hesitated. I could tell she didn't want to go on.

"What do they play with?"

"Nothing, really."

"Why do they call it football?

She took a deep breath. "Because they play for feet."

"Feet? What are talking about? How do you play for feet?" The answer came to me as soon as I asked it. "You mean feet?" "The teams are made up of ten Délon players and one human. The humans rotate as needed."

"As needed?" I asked.

"Until the other team gets his feet."

I cringed. "You mean the Délons cut off their feet."

"No." Lou shook her head. "That's against the rules. They can only hold the human down while..."

"While what?"

"While the human on the opposing team cuts off his or her feet."

"Her?"

"Welcome to a world with equal rights," she smiled. "Anyway, the team with the most feet at the end of four quarters wins."

"What human would do such a thing?"

"Needless to say, they don't have very long careers." She stood and took her plate to the kitchen sink. "In fact, there's only one human who's played the game since its inception who hasn't gotten so much as a scratch." She looked at me like I should know the answer.

"Who?"

She paused. She wanted me to come up with the answer on my own, but upon seeing my dumbfounded expression she blurted out, "Pepper Sands."

I stood up. "Pepper? No way. He wouldn't do such a thing." I sat back down when I realized he just might do such a thing. He was an animal as a linebacker who was known for taking great pleasure in inflicting pain on opposing players when he played professional football. But cutting off the foot of another human being? Could he actually do that? I pictured him the last time I saw him, hacking away at the Takers in our battle at the zoo. He was a great warrior.

"Don't think too badly of him," Lou said. "It's his job."

"His job?" I sat incredulous. "To cut off another man's foot?"

"Or woman's," Lou corrected.

"It's barbaric."

Lou reached out and touched my arm. "It's the way the world works now. It's not Pepper's fault. Besides they dope him up before each competition."

Mrs. Dayton began to clear the table.

"Here, let me help you, Mrs. Dayton," Lou said reaching for my plate.

Mrs. Dayton hissed and slapped Lou's hand away. At first, I thought it was just a playful gesture to let Lou know that she was a guest in Mrs. Dayton's house and that she didn't allow guests to clear the table, but when I got a look at her eyes I could see that it was something more. She didn't like Lou. I couldn't really blame her for not liking anybody or anything. Her tongue and hand had been cut off. What's to like?

Lou donned an apologetic expression and pulled her hand back. "Or I can just sit here. Whatever works for you."

Mrs. Dayton handed me a small pile of dirty plates and motioned for me to follow her. I shrugged my shoulders and obeyed. Lou gave me a "What's with her" look as I left the table. I shrugged my shoulders again.

At the sink, Mrs. Dayton ran the hot water. She picked up a bottle of liquid soap and squeezed it. Nothing came out. She squeezed harder. Still nothing. Exasperated, she approached Lou and forcefully tapped her on the shoulder. Startled, Lou stared at her. Mrs. Dayton pointed to the bottle and then pointed down.

She then motioned for Lou to leave the kitchen.

"I think she wants you to get some soap from the basement," I said.

Mrs. Dayton touched her nose and nodded.

"Oh, okay," Lou said. She stood. "Any place special I should look?"

Mrs. Dayton emphatically pointed down and escorted Lou to the door.

Lou looked at me with a puzzled expression and exited the kitchen.

Mrs. Dayton watched her move down the hallway and then quickly ran over to me. She pulled a small notepad and pen from a drawer near the sink. She laid the pad down and frantically began to write. When she was finished, she held the pad up for me to read.

"Leave," was all she wrote.

"Now," I said. "Don't you want help with the dishes?"

She shook her head and put the pad back down and wrote some more. When she finished she thumped the pad with her index finger.

I read. "Leave this world."

"This world?"

She wrote. "Not home."

"I know."

"No you don't." She was writing at break neck speeds. "The Source destroys home. You find Source and home is gone."

"Me? No, if I find the Source and destroy it, then the Délons are gone."

She huffed and stomped her foot. "You won't destroy it."

I was confused and just a little angry that she doubted my abilities. "I can do this. I know this sounds weird, but I'm a warrior. I beat the Takers..."

She shook her head. "Not won't because you can't. Won't because you won't want to."

I read the passage twice. "What? Yes I do."

She pointed to my left eye and carefully mouthed the word, "Marking." She then wrote. "You want what they want."

I shook my head. "No."

She nodded, and started to write more. I read over her shoulder. *"DON'T TRUST G..."*

We heard footsteps coming up the hallway. Mrs. Dayton stopped writing, frantically tore the pages out of the notepad and stuffed them in her pocket. She put her finger to her lips giving me the signal to keep quiet.

Lou entered the kitchen with a bottle of liquid soap. "Found it."

FIVE

Gordy was waiting for us outside Mrs. Dayton's house. He stood on the sidewalk hunched over and fidgety, hands clasped together in front of him, eyes drawn down. *"Don't Trust G,"* I thought.

Regardless, I was relieved to see him. I was ashamed to admit it, but once I underwent my marking, he was the furthest thing from my mind. I hadn't given one thought to whether he had become skinner food or not.

"Gord-o, good to see you," I said. I was feeling chipper despite Mrs. Dayton's warning. She was wrong. That was all there was to it. I didn't want what the Délons wanted. The marking's effect on me was temporary. I was the same old Oz Griffin that killed the Taker Queen. And Gordy was harmless.

"Oz," Gordy said with a nervous quiver. "You – you're looking good."

"I feel good." I turned to Lou. "This is my best pal, Gordy Flynn."

Lou shook his sweaty hand. "We met... kind of."

"Yeah." Gordy let out a breathless laugh. "In the principal's office. That was some weird stuff, huh?"

"About that," I said. "You know there was no way I was going to let that thing... you know, skin you, right?"

"Oh, sure, sure. I know," he said. "And you know that I was just about to kick some serious ass, right?"

"Sure, sure." I looked at Lou as she ducked her head to hide a smile. "Just like always." We turned up the sidewalk and headed toward my house. "So, what brings you this way, Gordy?"

"Nothing... you know. On my way to school... I was just wondering if we could hang... I mean I was wondering if it would be all right if I hung with you... you and Lou, I mean?" He was growing more and more nervous as he talked.

I stopped walking. The others quickly followed suit. "Gordy, what is up with you?"

"What do you mean?" he asked.

"You're like all nervous and shaky."

"I am?"

He looked at Lou. She confirmed my observation with a nod.

"Okay, maybe I am," he said. "But, dude, you're like king of those purple... things. How do you expect me to act?"

I thought about the question. He had a point. If I was in his position, I might be acting the same way. "I expect you to act like my friend."

He smiled. "Really? Cool. I was kind of afraid that you were all... you know... too kingy for me now. Plus, you were about to feed me to one of those skinner thingies yesterday..."

"I told you I wasn't going to let that happen," I said.

"Yeah, and I told you I was about to kick some major ass. People say things, you know."

I sighed. "Yeah, people say things." We started walking again. I remembered some of the thoughts I was having last night. Particularly my regrets for not letting the skinner have its way with Gordy. How could I have felt that way? "If you thought I was going to feed you to the skinner, why would you want to hang with me?"

He smiled. "I'm no idiot. You're the top dog, Ozzie. Ain't nobody going to mess with me if we're tight."

I should have been offended, but I wasn't. It was a smart move on his part. Gordy always had top-notch survival instincts. "That's cool," I said. "But you should know, I'm not planning on being king. You understand?"

"Dude, why not? Everybody will be falling all over themselves to treat you like... well, a king. You'd be a real dink to pass something like that up." He caught himself and cleared his throat. "Oh, I so did not mean that. Don't have me smited or nothing."

"Relax," I said. "It's me - Oz. I'm not into smiting. Besides to become king, I have to become Délon. I'm not really into the spider leg dreadlocks."

He laughed. "What other choice do you have? There're only two kinds of humans on this planet. Those who are about to become Délon and those who are about to become food. Call me crazy, but I'm not ready to be fitted for a happy meal suit. I'd rather be purple and evil than fleshy colored and delicious."

"You're forgetting the third kind of human," I said.

"Oh yeah, what's that?"

"The warrior who defeats the Délons and restores the planet to the way it was."

He shook his dead. "Oh, that kind - The kind that dies in a pointless show of heroism and bravery. Face it, Oz, the Délons are here to stay. You might as well join the party and get in on the fun."

I stopped and grabbed him by the scruff of his shirt. "Do you want to hang or not?"

"Dude, take it easy. I absolutely want to hang, man. I am here to serve you, your Oz-ship." He was back to his nervous self.

"Then shut up about the Délons."

"You got it." He put his hands up in the air as if he were surrendering. "Not another word about the purple people eaters."

I let him go and continued my walk. I noticed Lou hadn't

disputed anything Gordy had said. That made me madder at her than him. She had no right to lose faith. She knew what I was capable of - what we were capable of. I could beat the Délons, and she had no right to doubt me.

"So," Gordy said. "Why were you at the retard's house?"

I slugged him without warning. He stumbled backwards off the curb onto the street. Lou stepped in front of me.

"Don't," she said.

"What is up with you?" Gordy asked.

"I don't like that word," I said.

"Since when? You practically invented it." He was rubbing his jaw. Clearly, I didn't have the power I had the night before, otherwise I imagine Gordy would be lying dead on the street. The effects of the marking must have completely worn off.

He was right of course. I did use the word a lot. I teased Stevie Dayton with it on a daily basis until he cried. I was just as big a sinner as Gordy was, but that didn't change how I felt now. "I don't use it any more and, if you still want to hang, you better lose it from your vocabulary."

"It's done, man. I'll never say it again." He stepped back up on the sidewalk. "Friends?" He extended his hand.

I shook it with some hesitation. I didn't really like the new cowering Gordy, but he was still Gordy. It was kind of nice having him around because he reminded me of the world before crazy monsters took over. For the first time since I woke up in my bedroom, I thought about the others we used to run with. "Hey, where're Tim and Larry?"

"Haven't a clue," Gordy said. We turned up Westwood Avenue. "They disappeared about a month ago. I figured they were taken to the farm."

"The farm?" I asked.

Gordy looked past me and eyed Lou as we walked.

"He don't know about the farm?"

She shook her head sullenly.

"What's the farm?"

Gordy cleared his throat. "I told you, man. There ain't but two kinds of humans. Those that are about to become Délon and those that are about to become food."

"Yeah I get it. Skinner food, right?" I didn't like the direction this conversation was going.

He placed his hand on my shoulder as we walked. "Skinners ain't the only ones that use humans as food."

I walked in shocked despair. "What are you saying?"

"It ain't that complicated, Ozzie."

I looked at Lou. "They eat humans?"

She turned away from me and said. "They drink the blood."

"Blood?" I remembered my craving from the night before. When I felt fear, I craved the blood of a human. It was unmistakable. "Like vampires?"

"They say it's more like mosquitoes," Gordy said. "They don't drain ya'. They just drink until their bellies are full and move on."

"And this farm?"

Gordy picked up a rock and started tossing it from hand to hand. "They herd up the humans that they ain't planning on turning purple and keep them on a farm... I don't know if it's a farm, really. That's just what we call it. I hear they keep you fat and happy with sweets and soda and all kinds of pizza and junk food. But..." He stopped tossing the rock and fixated on it as if he was lost in a thought that he didn't want to find his way out of.

"But what?" I said.

He snapped out of his trance and started tossing the rock again. "It ain't no fun when they pick you as their cocktail for the evening. There's a lot of screaming and crying and praying for death." He cocked his right arm back and threw the rock at a car parked on the street, cracking the windshield. The look on his face was frustration and anger. I was an expert on those two emotions after my marking. I could spot them anywhere.

"You've seen it happen?" I asked.

He nodded. "I seen 'em do it to my mom. The ugly worms made me and my little sister watch. That's when I realized there were only two kinds of humans."

A horse whinnied in the distance. We heard the beating of hooves against the pavement. Through the trees and houses, I could see a horse and rider approaching from Crestwood. A horse with no rider followed. We stopped and watched as they turned up the other end of Westwood. At first, I wasn't sure I was seeing things right. The rider . . . it just couldn't be. I wiped my eyes and looked at Lou for confirmation. She was just as surprised as I was.

The rider was Roy. Not General Roy the Délon, but Roy the warrior. The one who had joined our gang on interstate 75 outside of Dalton, Georgia. The one who had fought with his sister to keep her in line, the one we had lost in the Georgia Dome.

He tapped Mr. Mobley lightly on the ribs with his heel and galloped up to our position. Lou and I stood motionless, mouths agape, trying to figure out what in the hell was going on.

"Friend of yours?" Gordy asked.

Neither Lou nor I answered. We simply couldn't believe our eyes.

Roy slowed Mr. Mobley to a walk when he got close enough to talk without shouting. "I brought an old friend." He motioned to the horse he was towing.

"Chubby," I said. The horse I had ridden to Atlanta. It was strange, but I was glad to see him. He wasn't my horse. He was just a mode a transportation I had used to get from point A to point B. Yet, there I was, absolutely giddy that he was back in my life. I walked over and stroked his long neck. For the moment, I had forgotten that Roy was Roy again.

"You want to go for a ride?" Roy asked.

I looked at him and then back at Lou and Gordy, still standing on the sidewalk. Lou was still mystified by Roy's sudden reappearance.

"We got to get to school, Oz," Gordy said.

Roy laughed. "School's over for Oz."

"What? No way," Gordy said.

"Kings have very little need for school." Roy's face began to vibrate.

"What about king sidekicks?" Gordy asked. "I can't see how school does us much good, either."

Roy breathed deeply. He was trying to control something inside of him. His face twitched and his eyes bulged. "What is this sidekick business?" Roy struggled to ask me.

"Tell him, Oz," Gordy interjected. "We're tight, you and me. I'm his main man, his numero uno, his bench strength..."

"Gordy," I said.

"I'm the head cheese in his cheese... collection. The sugar in his cup... no wait, that didn't come out right," Gordy said.

"Gordy," I said again, a little louder, a little more forcefully.

"The important thing to know is that I'm not skinner bait or farm material because me and his royal kingship are like toast and jam, okay," Gordy continued nervously. "We're like salt and pepper. Wherever there's one there is the other..."

"Gordy, shut up!" I said. I mounted Chubby. "Lou, can you look after him?"

She reluctantly nodded. "You sure you'll be okay."

I looked at Roy who had gotten his twitching face under control. "I'll be fine."

Délon City

***

We rode for a half mile without saying a word. I had never seen Tullahoma from the back of a horse. The view was somehow different. It was purer, more utopian than it was from the window of a fast moving automobile. It smelled of pine and late fall. Taking in the sites of the small southern hamlet from the saddle made me feel whole. I didn't know why, and quite frankly, I didn't question it. I just enjoyed it.

Roy broke the silence. "It's beautiful, isn't it?"

I didn't answer right away. I wasn't sure beautiful was the right word. I wasn't sure it was a big enough word. "A little more than that," I said.

He smiled. "I know what you mean."

"This is why you don't travel by car?"

He nodded. "You can't feel the land from a car. They're necessary. That's the only reason we allow them, but they're not for Délons."

I turned to him. His face twitched some more. It looked as if it would hop from his skull at any moment. "This is a trick, isn't it?"

"Huh?" He touched his face. "Oh, this. I just thought this face would please you more." I thought back to the Georgia Dome when Pepper's man, Shaw, had morphed into a Délon right before our eyes. "Personally, it disgusts me. If you wish, I could return to my true self."

"No," I said. "I prefer this."

"As you wish," he answered.

We rode in silence a few minutes longer. I strained to observe him out of the corner of my eye without him noticing. At one point, I saw a spider leg emerge from his wind blown brown hair. It was more disturbing than seeing countless dozens of them dancing on top of his head.

He broke the silence again. "You can't go home."

I looked over my shoulder towards my house and then back at him. "Why? What's going on at my house...?"

"That's not what I mean," he said. "You can't go back to the way it was. I know you think you can, but you can't."

I swallowed hard and mulled over what he was telling me. "Why exactly am I supposed to believe you?"

"You are trying to change the nature of things..."

"The nature of things," I laughed. "There is nothing natural about this place. It's all a twisted fantasy of some poor mentally handicapped guy in New Jersey because jerks like me wouldn't let him have a moment's peace and live with some dignity."

This time he laughed. "Cruelty is the heartbeat of nature."

"What's that supposed to mean?"

"To be cruel is to be true to nature. A lion does not tenderly tear a zebra's belly open and feed. It stalks it and chases it and sinks its teeth into the zebra's neck until it chokes the life out of it. The strong feed on the weak. That is the way of nature."

I snickered. "In case you haven't noticed, I'm not a zebra."

"No," he smiled. "You're a lion. You fed on Stevie Dayton, ripped the hope and self-worth from him as efficiently as any carnivore has ripped the entrails from its prey."

His words stung me like a hive of angry wasps. I wanted to deny it, to scream at him, to demand that he take it back, but I couldn't. As much as I hated to hear it, it was the truth. He was right. I knew it. I had even admitted it to myself over and over again, but hearing it out loud, spoken with such clarity and admiration made me sick to my stomach. I was a Délon before Délons even existed.

"You spend too much time denying your true nature," Roy said. "You are not just one of us." He chuckled. "You are the reason for us.

"Is this why you asked me to ride with you, to make me feel like crap for what I've done?"

"On the contrary. I'm trying to make you feel proud."

I dug my heels into Chubby's ribs and whistled. "Get up, boy." Chubby went into a trot and we pulled away from Roy and Mr. Mobley. I didn't want to hear any more.

Roy put Mr. Mobley into a trot and it wasn't long before the horses were matching each other stride for stride. "I've upset you," Roy said.

"Go away."

"I'm leaving for Délon City this afternoon."

"Good for you."

"Tomorrow, you will do the same. You will have a horse and supplies for the trip." His left eye turned white as he spoke.

"Alone?"

"Not quite. Devlin will travel with you."

I kicked Chubby again. His stride turned into a gallop. Again, Mr. Mobley quickly matched our pace. "And Lou?"

"She will go with us..."

"She goes with me," I said.

His hair was replaced with the spider legs. He wanted to deny me my request, but he didn't. "Fine, and I suppose the curly haired one will be joining you..."

"Gordy? Yeah why not." With that I gave Chubby another kick in the ribs and he bounded into a full out sprint. Mr. Mobley quickly chased after his equestrian counterpart, and we were racing neck and neck. I glanced over at Roy. His humanity had completely disappeared. He was General Roy again. Apparently, disguising oneself as a human took a lot of energy and concentration. He couldn't sustain it for very long.

Much as I tried not to, I was enjoying myself. Riding Chubby, racing Roy and Mr. Mobley felt liberating. I was in a miserable place with miserable freaks that sucked on humans for blood and turned the rest of humanity into freaks like them, yet all I could think about was how much fun I was having on the back of that damn horse. I was deathly afraid of horses not long ago (or was it long ago, it was hard to keep up with the missing time), but there I was not wanting to ever have to dismount.

"You ride like a king," General Roy shouted.

Upon hearing those words, I pulled back on the reigns, and quickly brought Chubby to a stop. General Roy rode a few feet farther and then did the same. He circled Mr. Mobley around and walked him toward me.

"We're not friends," I said.

"Kings have no friends," he answered. "Just servants."

"I'm not your king." I turned Chubby around and trotted back toward Lou and Gordy. "I'm your enemy." This time Roy did not follow. I could feel his dead eyes staring at me as I rode away. His anger burned. I could hear it crackling in my head. He meant to kill me, some time, somewhere. I wasn't sure if even he knew it, but the desire was deep inside him. Eventually it would be too much for him to ignore.

***

Gordy and Lou were waiting for me at the back door to my house. I jumped off Chubby's back feeling invigorated from the ride.

"Didn't know you could ride," Gordy said.

"Hope you can," I said.

"Me, why?"

"We're going to Délon City tomorrow."

"We? Dude, on a horse?" Gordy was so nervous he was

almost shaking.

"Me, too?" Lou asked.

"Yeah Devlin will be joining us..." As soon as the words came out of my mouth Délon Devlin stepped out the back door.

"That's right. I've got to babysit you twerps all the way to Délon City. One wrong move from any of you and you're skinner food. You comprehend me?" He shoved Gordy in the back and stepped onto the bricked walkway.

"Gotcha', cuz," Gordy said. "No wrong moves here."

"Were you always this spineless or do I bring out the best in you?" Devlin asked Gordy.

"It's all you, big guy," Gordy answered. "All you."

Devlin grabbed Lou by the face and pulled her close. "How 'bout you, female, do you fear me?"

Without thinking, I ran and kicked Devlin in the back of the knees as hard as I could. He fell hard to the ground. "Hands off, Devlin."

Hearing him groan in pain and watching him struggle to stand back up, I suddenly became very afraid. I had hurt him. No good could come from that. As far as the Délons were concerned, I was their future king, but they didn't have much in the way of self-control. If I got them mad enough, any one of them would rip me apart without a second thought.

Devlin huffed and growled like a tiger. The insect mandibles shot from his mouth and snapped wildly. His hands balled into fists. I feared this was the end for me. He stepped toward me and stopped. His spider leg hairdo reached for me, but quickly retracted. In a remarkable show of restraint, he backed away.

"You shouldn't push me," he said.

"Looks like we both have rules." My voice began to crack. "You follow mine, I'll follow yours. Deal?"

"No deal," he hissed. "You follow mine, you live. You don't..."

He threw a fist into the brick exterior of the house and punched a hole in it. "That clear?" he said extracting his hand from the side of my house.

"Clear," I said.

"Good." He turned and headed for the street. "Your pig of a mother has eaten all the screamers. I have to feed before I lose all my strength." He disappeared around the corner.

"You're nuts," Gordy cried. "Super nuts!"

"I wasn't thinking," I said. "You okay, Lou?"

"I can take care of myself," she said.

"I know. I just... I don't know what came over me."

"You're in love," Gordy said. "That's what came over you."

I was stunned by the accusation. "In love? I am not."

"He is not in love with me," Lou insisted. "Take that back."

"I saw what I saw," Gordy said.

"Take it back," I said stepping toward him.

"Okay, whatever. You're not in love. Geesh, chill out. I was just saying..."

"Well, don't just say, got it?"

"Got it."

I walked up the steps to the back door and went in the house. Gordy let Lou pass with his hands in the air and then followed her through the door.

"Ma," I yelled. I stopped when I noticed her solifipod looked different. A reddish slime oozed from the top and dripped to the floor.

"I hate those things," Lou said. "They give me the willies."

"You and me both," I said.

"The shunter's been out," Gordy said.

"How do you know?" I asked.

"I can tell," he answered. "I've seen enough of those things to suit me for a hundred lifetimes."

Délon City

"What is a shunter?" I asked.

"Dude, you don't want to know," he said.

"He's right," Lou added. "Consider yourself lucky you don't know."

"But..." before I could say another word, my mom rounded the corner. She was in an almost zombie like state dressed in her pajamas, the same reddish substance on the solifipod covered her clothes and neck. Dozens of puncture wounds outlined her face.

"Mom?"

She looked at me, or through me is more like it. "I'm hungry." Her voice was thick and unsteady. "Do you have something I can eat?"

"No... maybe there's something in the kitchen." I moved past her and headed for the refrigerator.

"Everything in there is dead," she protested.

I turned to her, my eyes struggling to take the site of her in, my ears throbbing from hearing what she'd just said.

"I need to feel it squirming in my mouth. Crying in pain. I need to feel it die."

"Mom..."

"Forget it, dude," Gordy said. "Your mom's had her brain punctured. She's gone."

Mom zeroed in on Gordy's voice. "Do you taste good, human?"

Gordy stepped back. "Me? No way. I'm sour as all get out. I eat nothing but... you know, sour stuff."

"I like sour," Mom said.

"Dude, your mom is really starting to creep me out." Gordy backed away.

"I just want a little taste."

Pop came rushing in from the bedroom wearing his robe. The purple rash that had been limited to a spot on his wrist and neck had grown to cover about sixty percent of his body. "Sorry, sorry," he said. "She got away from me." He wrapped his arm around her shoulder. "Come along, Sharon. We need to get you dressed."

"What's wrong with her?" I asked.

"Nothing," Pop said. "I just need to get her to transformation therapy. The first night with the shunter is always draining. The little buggers don't know when to stop. The therapist will have her feeling right as rain in no time."

"Feed me the living!" she screamed.

"Later, dear," Pop said. He rushed her out of the living room and into the hallway toward the bedroom.

There was a long period of awkward silence between Lou, Gordy, and me as we all tried to decipher my mom's bizarre behavior.

Gordy finally broke the silence. "Dude, crazy much?"

Lou slapped his arm. "That was rude."

"What? His mom has stepped way out on the loony limb. That's all I'm saying. I mean I've seen the shunted before and they were never that..."

"Wacko," I said.

"Exactly."

Lou stomped her foot and put her left hand on her hip. "Trust me, I have seen way worse. I've been the guest of momma and poppa Délon for a while now, and they have shown me some wild and wacky stuff. Do you know I actually saw a shunter crush the skull of a human host..."

She stopped when she realized what she was saying. The expression on my face must have terrified her because she turned a brilliant shade of white. She had been exposed to the ways of the Délons for so long that witnessing the brutal death of another human meant nothing to her. It was scary to see the apathy in

Délon City

her eyes. "What am I saying? Your mom is going to be fine. God, I hate this world. I hate it. I hate it. I hate it."

"That's all right," I said.

"No, it's not," she answered. "That was stupid of me." She flopped down on the couch. "You should know. The shunter that crushed the guy's skull was a black market shunter. It wasn't matched to the host through the normal process. Some people are just so anxious to be Délons they try to take shortcuts. They have no idea what they're dealing with."

"I don't get why anyone would want to be a Délon," I said sitting in my Pop's recliner.

"Power, prestige," Gordy said staring out the window. "Same as it's always been. Only now you gotta be purple to be a player."

"Are people really that desperate?" I asked.

"In a word," Gordy laughed, "Absolutely."

"It's more than that," Lou said. "People are scared. Think about it, we were at the top of the food chain for a long time. We called the shots for almost every living thing on the planet. We were in control. That all changed in the blink of an eye. People are so desperate to reclaim their superiority they're willing to stop being people."

Gordy sat on the other end of the couch. "Like I said you gotta be purple to be a player." He closed his eyes. I could feel the heaviness of sleep starting to smother him.

Lou's eyelids started to droop. She smiled and let them fall shut. The energy I had awoken with was gone. An achy sleep started to overtake me. I fought it. I don't know why, but it felt wrong. I had a world to save. There was no time for sleep.

*****

My next recollection was foggy. I'm not sure if it was a dream

71

or not. But somewhere in that state between sleep and consciousness, I heard my Mom and Pop leave the house. Mom was still droning on about being hungry for something alive. Pop grew more and more impatient as he tried to quiet her and get her out of the house. My eyes were closed but I could see them in my mind's eye. Pop, dressed in his usual work attire, one arm around Mom, who was dressed in jeans and a baby blue sweater coat that hung to her knees, her hair unkempt as far as Mom's old standards. Pop's other hand was digging in his pocket looking for his keys. He wanted her to tell her to shut up about being hungry, but he didn't.

They exited the house, him gently nudging her out the door and pulling it closed behind them. I heard the key slide into the lock and turn to the left. Their heads passed the window as they headed for the garage.

The truck backed out of the garage and down the driveway, turning left on Westwood. They drove out of my thoughts.

As I began to draw my thoughts backwards, the vision of Westwood Avenue began to fade into blackness. The faint image of another vehicle coming down the road caught my attention. It was a green and yellow 1972 VW bus.

SIX

Isprang out of the recliner and raced to the window. Only I didn't really because I was already at the window. Or did I? Had I been nodding off to sleep, or had I actually seen my Mom and Pop leave the house? Lou and Gordy were out cold. I looked out the window. The green and yellow VW bus was just arriving.

An echo of a voice sounded off in my head. "Let's just say time doesn't really make much sense any more. It kind of jumps all over the clock..." That's what Lou had said at Stevie Dayton's house. It was the only answer. I had experienced a time jump.

I shook off my muddled mindset and bolted out the front door of my house. The round little van idled on the street as I ran towards it. Clouds of gray smoke billowed from the exhaust. One thought shot out from the back of my mind. Was I still asleep or was this real?

I could see the outline of the driver. He sat, both hands on the wheel, one chin resting on top of another, a ball cap positioned on his round head, the bill just 10 or so degrees from sitting at a 90 degree angle.

The harder I ran, the farther I got from the van. This was a dream. There was no other explanation.

The engine revved. The putt-putt-putt of the ancient foreign-made cylinders crept out from the back of the fat little bus. The smell of burning propane filled the air. It was Wes's little van. That was no longer in question. The only thing left to determine was if this was just a cruel, taunting movie being played out in my head while I slept, or was this... could I dare to hope that it was real.

"Wes!" I yelled.

The driver honked. The weak unthreatening sound of it was almost laughable. The absurdity was too much. Wes was proudly redneck - NASCAR watching, tobacco chewing, beer drinking, football loving redneck to the very core. Yet, there he sat in his custom made 1972 VW green and yellow bus with a horn that sounded like it belonged on a tricycle. It was like watching a bear take the SATs. It just wasn't right.

I finally made headway. Twenty feet from the van, I could see Wes's yellow-toothed green. He tapped the bill of his cap. In an instant, his face was blacked out by something climbing in the passenger seat from the back of the bus. My eyes and mind adjusted. The something had fur . . . a tricolor coat, pointed ears, long powerful muzzle.

I stopped, concentrated, forced focused my disbelieving eyes. "Kimball?" I said, or may not have said. The shock of it displaced me - my actions, my inactions, all rolled up into one gigantic memory. I did everything and nothing in that moment.

The dog in the passenger seat barked.

"Kimball!" I screamed. This time I knew I had spoken out loud. I could feel the sound vibrate every inch of my body. My dog was alive. Wes was alive. The ugly green and yellow VW bus was even alive. "Kimball!"

"Oz?" A distant voice rang out.

I ignored it and started to run again.

"Oz?"

I turned to see Lou standing by the couch. "You okay?" she asked.

I was once again standing at the window. I watched as Pop's truck pulled out of the driveway.

Délon City

"I'm not dreaming," I said.

"What?" Lou approached.

The sputtering engine of the VW bus came roaring down the street.

"They're alive." This time I ran out the back door, and mounted Chubby. With a kick and flip of the reigns, he turned and bounded down the driveway. I didn't look back to see if Lou had followed. I didn't have to. I could feel her watching me at the window as I galloped toward the street.

The van streaked by the house. I steered Chubby after it. The sometimes clunky stride of the steed became silky smooth. His powerful head bobbed effortlessly as we caught up with the sputtering bus. In no time, I was looking in the driver side window at my old friend Wes.

He smiled. "'Bout time, kid," he yelled over the sounds of his engine and my panting horse. "'Bout damn time."

"Is it really you?" I cried.

He laughed. "What kind of fool question is that? Course it's me."

"Kimball?"

My dog stuck his head out from the back of the van and barked.

I wanted to cry I was so happy. "Pull over."

"Can't," Wes snarled. "They're on me like a June bug on a shrub."

I looked around. There was no one in sight. "I don't see anybody."

"They don't much care to be seen, but trust me, they're there." He pulled up a plastic Pepsi bottle he had nestled between his legs and spit in it. A dark chunk of saliva dripped down inside. "Meet me at the mattress store at midnight."

"The mattress store?"

"You ain't forgot, have ya'?" he asked. I could see the tobacco pinched between his lower lip and gums.

"No," I said.

He nodded. "You best pull back now. I gotta skedaddle."

I let Chubby sprint for a little while longer. I couldn't take my eyes off Kimball. I didn't want to let him or Wes out of my sight.

"Kid," Wes said, "it's all right. Just be at the mattress store tonight at midnight."

With that, I pulled back on Chubby's reigns and watched the 1972 green and yellow VW bus race down to the end of Westwood and onto Lincoln Street.

***

"Was that...?" Lou stopped herself from asking a question she thought ridiculous. She had seen the van. She knew that it was Wes's, but to assume that Wes was actually driving it just seemed too much to hope for.

I stood in my living room looking over her and Gordy, not knowing what to say. Inside, I was jumping for joy. Hell, it was like midnight on New Year's eve in my head, but something inside of me, a distant ungraspable knowing, told me to keep this to myself. Still, the urge to share my excitement was almost too much to bear. "It was..." I started, but stopped. A vision popped in my head.

I stood in a darkened warehouse. Shattered wooden crates were strewn throughout the dingy space. I was covered in the red blood of humans and the purple blood of Délons. In my hand was my old sword, J.J. I wielded it with a weakened grip. In one corner of the room, Gordy was being tortured and maimed by a creature I did not recognize. It was opaque and covered in a sheen of mucus. It stood on four crab-like legs. Its upper body appeared human. Its head rested on its neck upside down. Its eyes were where its mouth should be, and its mouth, sewn shut in a wilted frown, was on its forehead. It had two hands with five willowy fingers each that ended in railroad-sized spikes.

I attempted to turn to help Gordy, but something lay across my feet. I looked down and saw the bloodied body of Lou, a puncture wound to her chest. I had killed her.

With a painful rip, the vision disappeared from my mind. My mouth went dry, and my knees wobbled. "Don't tell them!" a voice raged in my head. "Don't you dare tell them!"

"It . . . wasn't who you think it was," I said in a reedy voice.

Lou's eyes narrowed, and she bowed her head. "Of course it wasn't." The disappointment in her voice was palpable.

"Wasn't who?" Gordy asked.

"An old friend," I answered. I couldn't look at him without seeing him being thrashed by the creature in my vision. "Listen, Gordy, maybe you should... go home."

"What? Why?" He sounded hurt and anxious all at once.

"I just don't think it's a good idea for you to be around me..."

He cut me off. "What is this? You said I could hang. You said we were friends again. What you're like king now and you don't need old Gordy around any more? Is that it?"

"No," I said. "It's just not safe..."

"Safe?" He laughed. "Safe went out the window when our purple friends showed up!"

"Bad things tend to happen when I'm around," I said raising my voice above his. I was trying to save the poor slob's life, and he was throwing a hissy fit.

"When you're around?" He laughed again. Not a real laugh, but an angry, disgusted guttural release of air from the pit of his stomach. "Were you around when they beat the crap out of my old man and sucked the blood out of my mom? Were you around when they fed my little sister to a pack of skinners? Were you around when they marked me?"

I looked at him struggling to say something – anything that didn't make me an even bigger jerk.

"Yeah that's right, jackass, I've been marked!" He was shrieking now. Spit was coming out of the corners of his mouth. He was angry and confused and scared. "This isn't just about you! Bad stuff has happened to all of us! If you don't want me around because I cramp your king... ness, then fine, but don't pretend you're trying to protect me because there's nowhere I'm safer than with you!" He started to cry, a shoulder quaking, snot flopping, shallow breathing type of cry.

Lou put her arm around his shoulder and helped him sit back down on the sofa. "He's right," she said. She hesitated and then spoke again. "We saw it, too."

"Saw it? The vision?" I was stunned and ashamed.

"It wasn't a vision." She rocked with Gordy and patted his back. She looked at me, eyes steady and penetrating. "It was the future."

"The future?" I backed away.

"I should say, a future. Happening now..."

"A time jump," I said.

She nodded.

"But I would never... do that to you." I couldn't say the word "kill" out loud.

She released Gordy from her comforting embrace and stood. She approached me with a relentless seriousness in her face. "Listen to me," she barked. "You do whatever it takes to get the world back to the way it was. Do you understand me?"

"But..."

"No! No buts!" This isn't a game. None of us are more important than our final objective!"

Délon City

"I'm not killing anyone!" I shouted.

Délon Devlin entered the house chewing on a wriggling screamer. He held a paper bag full of the wormy munchables in his hand. He felt the heat from our exchange and chuckled. "What's wrong? You kiddies can't decide which cartoon to watch?"

I backed away from Lou and headed toward my room. "What time will the rest of the horses be here?"

Devlin swallowed his screamer. "In the morning, sixish."

"See that nobody disturbs me until then," I said.

Devlin looked bemused. "Are you giving me an order?"

I stopped at the door and turned to him. I was flummoxed by my little exchange with Lou and I was in no mood for Devlin's crap. "Look, let's stop playing this stupid game. I'm your king, like it or not. The fact that I don't have purple skin and a spider leg afro are just formalities. So, unless you want my first official act as your dead-eyed lord and master to have your head shaved and your tongue ripped out by Canter, then just do what I say, and save us all a lot of trouble!"

Devlin dithered. He looked at Lou and Gordy. They were just as surprised by my behavior as he was. He looked back at me and, after some consideration, meekly said, "Okay."

I shut the door to my room, and cried the same shoulder quaking, snot flopping, shallow breathing cry that Gordy had cried. But unlike him, I didn't have the courage to do it out loud.

***

After nightfall, I crawled out of my window and silently guided Chubby through the yard into our neighbor's, the Drucker's, backyard. There was a time that they would have immediately stormed out of their house and ran to my mother and father, demanding that my parents punish me for trespassing on their

79

perfect lawn of Bermuda grass. Instead, Mr. Drucker, a round little man with thinning blonde hair and thick black-rimmed glasses, smiled a phony smile from his living room window as I passed. Mrs. Drucker, purple complexion, grayish hair mixed with spider legs, eyes not quite dead, stood beside him holding a live mouse by the tail. Dinner.

I climbed on top of Chubby and began my journey to Manchester. I had not thought about Wes's mattress shop for a long time. It was a nice end-of-the-world setup, situated next to a grocery store, not far from a Wal-Mart. You had a nice place to lay your head at night, your choice of an assortment of nonperishable food items, and the company was pretty good.

As I rode, I wondered how different things would be if we had decided to stay in that little mattress store and not tried to set things right by destroying the Takers. The Takers were mindless brutes. Not a group you'd have over for Christmas dinner, but as far as soulless, evil rulers of the planet, they were a lot better than the Délons.

From out of nowhere I heard *"DON'T TRUST G"* in my head. Gordy was a scared, sometimes spineless little kid, but he was still my friend. We had a history together that went back to before we could both walk and feed ourselves. If there was anyone left on this planet I could still trust, it was him. Then my vision, or leap to the future, came back to me. He was being tortured by some thing, some horrible thing. I was turning to help him... The image became clearer. My hand, the one holding J.J., was covered in a flaky purple rash. I wasn't turning to help Gordy. I was turning to help the creature, the horrible crab-legged creature with the upside down face, finish Gordy off.

I was the one who couldn't be trusted. I would betray my friends. Mrs. Dayton knew it. I wanted what they wanted, the Délons...

Délon City

"No," I whispered. I refused to believe it. How had Lou put it? "A future." It was a possibility, not the only possibility. I could change it. I could take a different path... A hopeless thought crept into my head. I had no idea what path led me to that future. How could I change the mistakes that would lead me there if I didn't know what the mistakes were?

When I reached highway 55, I began to notice a presence, a whisper of an apparition hiding in the wind. Shadows from the half-moon lit sky seemed to chase me as I rode past a cemetery. I could feel someone or something watching me.

Instinctively, I reached for my weapon, J.J., even though I had not seen it in days (or months, according to Lou). It was lost... A sudden rush of relief came over me. It was lost. J.J. was gone. I couldn't kill Lou with J.J. if I didn't have the sword.

My relief was momentary. A sound drifted in from the darkness. It was a rattling or a low steady... chatter. The Takers' calling card. They were back. A massive creature crept over the sloping hills of the cemetery. It plodded toward me. I gave Chubby a kick to send him into a speedy getaway, but he reared instead. Ahead of us, a second mass of darkness approached. Its silhouette was unmistakable, the pointed ears, the long dangling arms, the ridiculous wide expanse of the shoulders. It was a Taker.

I pulled Chubby's reigns to the left to make our escape and saw two more Takers appear from the thicket of trees and shrubs that bordered the northbound side of the highway. I looked to the rear and saw another dozen or so Takers advancing. We were surrounded.

"I know it doesn't look good, boy," I told Chubby, "but we've got to pick a direction."

As if he understood me, Chubby lurched forward and sped south toward Manchester. Not only was it the direction of our final destination, it left us with only one Taker to elude. I was beginning to believe that Chubby was a lot smarter than your average horse.

The Taker crouched as we drew closer. It extended its arms and flashed its ruddy eyes. Thirty feet away, I could see its sprawling toothy mouth set in a frightening smile. It shook its head violently.

I looked over my shoulder to see if the others were following. They were and ever faster.

"Okay, Chub," I said. "Time to kick it into high gear!" The tiger horse responded. I could feel his muscles tighten as he ran faster than he ever had before.

The Taker in front of us snarled as we came within mere feet of it. Chubby deftly shifted to the right just outside the grasp of the Taker's razor sharp claws. The slobbering beast wheeled on the balls of its enormous feet and gave pursuit. Its long, thumping stride shook the ground. In a saliva spraying fit, the Taker released a gurgled roar.

Chubby ran harder, but not faster. The horse was working itself up into a foamy lather. I could feel its heart pounding through the saddle. A sense of panic soared through me, as Chubby snorted and panted toward Manchester.

The Taker we passed was gaining on us too easily. In another step or two, it could leap on Chubby's back and start ripping me to shreds with its meaty hands.

"C'mon, Chub-boy, c'mon!" The old horse gave me one more burst of energy. We were flying across the pitted pavement. Ahead of us to the right was the shopping center with the mattress store. "Just a little more, boy. Just a little more."

Of course, I didn't know what we were going to do once we reached the mattress store. The Taker wouldn't disappear just because we reached where we were going. He wasn't an escort to make sure we made it to our final destination safely. He was a hunter looking for food, and we were the food.

Délon City

Chubby dipped into the parking lot. The Kroger's grocery store that made up most of the shopping center was dark. It was closed for the night, and the employees had long since vacated the premises. The little mattress store at the end wasn't just closed for the night. It was boarded up, out of business. Wes's VW bus was nowhere to be seen. We were running to nothing.

I looked over my shoulder. The Taker was gone. I stared back in anguished disbelief. Anguished because my horse and I had been driven to near coronaries over the thought of what the greasy monster might do to us if it caught us, and the damn thing didn't even have the decency to keep up its pursuit. It had a duty as a creature of the night to keep on our heels and drive us to either incredible feats of bravery or cowardice. That's what monsters do.

I gently pulled back on Chubby's reigns. The exhausted horse didn't want to slow down at first. Eventually he slipped into a gallop and then a trot until his aching legs gave way to a traipsing walk.

I jumped off his back and fought the urge to throw up. I had not run an inch, yet I was so short of breath I thought I might pass out.

Why were the Takers here? I had killed the queen. That was supposed to be the end of them.

I heard a whacking sound, as if a wooden pole had fallen to the concrete surface of the parking lot. It came from the direction of the mattress store.

"Wes?" I cried between heaving breaths.

Chubby whinnied and snorted.

"Wes?"

Nothing.

I inched forward, keeping my eyes on the mattress shop. I thought I could hear the sputtering of the little VW engine coming from the poorly lit corner of the shopping center. It was Wes. It had to be.

Slowly, I pulled Chubby toward the entrance of the mattress shop. He protested and thrashed his head back. "C'mon, boy. We can't stand here all night, and I'm sure as heck not going back the way we came."

The horse snorted one last exasperated sigh and unenthusiastically let me guide him toward the sound of the sputtering.

As we got closer, the sputtering didn't seem to sound like sputtering anymore. It sounded amazingly similar to chattering. I swallowed. My throat was dry, and my eyes were watery. My ears closed up and all I could hear was the thump-thump-thump of my overtaxed heart. Each step I took was a huge effort. It pained me each time it was necessary for me to take another.

At the door, I dropped Chubby's reigns. "If anything should happen, Chubs, run." I looked into his big brown eyes and could tell that would not be a problem.

As I passed the mattress shop, I peered in the window and saw my reflection. I was white as a ghost. My hair was ratty and my slim frame was barely imposing enough to cast a reflection.

Chubby shrieked and reared. I turned to him. "What's wrong?"

Looking back in the window I saw Chubby's front hooves touch back down on the ground. Just nerves. The steed was understandably jumpy. After all we had just had a run in with a... Taker.

In the window, I could see a line of Takers behind me. Twenty or so, all crouched down on their haunches, teeth bared, claws foreword. Standing fully erect, they would range in height from eight to fifteen feet. I slowly turned. Only the sounds of their snapping jaws interrupted the incessant chattering. Chubby reared and kicked his front feet. This seemed to confuse the Takers. That's when I remembered that Takers could only see humans. They couldn't see animals. Chubby was safe.

I was not, however. There was no point in me running. They would be on top of me before I could get ten feet. Killed by Takers. That was one way to make sure I did not betray my friends and become the Délon king. I stepped forward. Chubby moved in front of me.

"Get back, boy."

The spotted tiger horse paid no attention to me. He stomped toward the line of Takers. He seemed to realize they couldn't see him. They blindly stepped back.

"Chubby," I yelled. "Get out of here!"

The horse refused. He turned and side-stepped toward the Takers. The monsters flailed their arms and growled.

A pack of dogs bounded from the corner of the mattress store. Their barks shrieked through the night. The lead dog was Kimball. Eight dogs similar in size and stature followed him. They varied in color from white to blonde to black and every imaginable combination of those colors.

Instead of bolting in fear, the Takers calmed and stood at attention. The dogs circled, barking and nipping at the great beasts. They weren't attacking them. They were wrangling them.

"Get 'em up, dogs!" I heard a familiar voice shout. Wes stepped out from behind the mattress store.

"Wes?"

He smiled at me. "Got them Greasywhoppers just where I want 'em, kid." He whistled and the pack of dogs moved the herd of Takers through the parking lot and behind the mattress store.

"Them things is dumb as washboards," Wes laughed. "Can't for the life of me remember why we was so damned scared of

85

'em." He stepped toward me, his smile a mile wide. "Damn fine to see ya', son." He bent down and picked me up in a smothering bear hug.

"What's going on?" I asked between labored breaths.

"C'mon," he said putting me down. "There's some folks who want to see you."

***

When we entered the back of the mattress store, I heard the playful prattling of children. The sound of a girl giggling wildly struck me as odd given the place and circumstances.

I heard a young boy cry out, "No fair, Val! You can't use both hands!"

Tucked away in the front corner of the store, sitting behind a musky smelling display mattress, a young boy and girl thumb wrestled.

"Valerie? Tyrone?"

They turned in my direction. "Oz!" they screamed in unison and bolted toward me.

The youngest of my warriors were now a year older and about four inches taller between them.

"It's you," I said. "It's really you." We locked in a three-way hug in the middle of the store.

"Ozzie, my man," Tyrone said in a voice that was much deeper than I remembered. "Wes said you were alive, but we didn't believe him."

"I did," Valerie insisted. "I knew nothing could kill Oz."

"You're such a liar," Tyrone grunted.

"I'm not..."

"Hush up," Wes barked. "Don't you two start your squabbling again. You'll drive a body crazy with that nonsense."

86

Délon City

They curbed their inclination to bicker, and took a seat on a nearby mattress. I couldn't stop looking at them. The last time I had seen them was at Zoo Atlanta. They were frightened, but brave. We all were.

I heard a bark just seconds before a hundred pound German shepherd tackled me. He covered my face with wet doggie kisses. "Kimball," I laughed. "Down, boy."

I sat up on my elbows and surveyed the lot of them. They were all here. I wouldn't have dared to let myself believe it if I hadn't seen it with my own eyes, but there they were. "Is this real?" I heard myself asking.

"Real as real can be," Wes said.

"But... how?" I climbed up on a nearby mattress.

"Well, things got a little hairy after you killed the Taker Queen," Wes said. "The Délons swooped down on us quicker than a hiccup. They got Miles and Devlin right off. There weren't nothing we could do to help 'em. Old Doc Hollis was next, and then I seen Pepper take four of those purple boogers out before they dragged him off."

"What about you guys?"

"Well, they would of got us for sure if hadn't been for the big guy." Wes motioned over his shoulder to the back of the room.

Stepping out of the shadows was an enormous beast, similar to the Takers except it had white hair. The monster stooped over to keep from hitting its head on the ceiling.

"Tarak?"

"Son of Zareh," the white beast said.

Stepping out from behind the creature's left leg, his tiny hands gripping tightly to Tarak's white hair, was a drooling toddler.

My heart stopped. "Nate?"

SEVEN

I found myself not being able to believe where I was, what I was seeing, who was sitting around me. It was a hallucination, a trick of some kind. My army, my warriors, minus a soldier or two, sat staring at me, waiting for me to speak. But what do you say to ghosts? That's what they had to be.

Kimball licked my hand, and I pulled back, startled. I tentatively touched him.

"He's real," Tarak said, his voice as intimidating and unsettling as ever. His massive frame was nearly crushing the bed he was sitting on. "We all are."

"I know," I said not knowing if I really believed it. "It's just that..." I hesitated and scanned the faces of everybody in the room. "How?"

"I told ya'," Wes said. "Tarak here saved our butts."

I looked at Tarak. "I thought you said this was our war to fight."

He sighed. "It was. And you won, but the war with the Délons is for a different warrior and a different Keeper. You've done your part."

"What do you mean a different warrior?"

"There are seven Storytellers. That means seven stories with seven sets of warriors, seven Keepers, and seven races of destroyers."

"Destroyers?" I said. "What is this? Who made up these rules?"

Délon City

Tarak thought about the question. "I don't know. They have always been."

"Are you telling me that there is another band of warriors out there who are going through what we went through last time?"

"I am."

"Who is it? Where are they?"

Tarak's expression soured. "You cannot know."

"What? Why?"

"Because those are the rules?"

"Stop with the rules," I shouted. "I know how to beat the Délons... I mean I think I do. I have to find these other warriors to let them know what I know."

"It is not allowed." Tarak said.

"Allowed..." The word shot out of my mouth with little control. I was tired of people (and mythical creatures) telling me what was and was not allowed. I was the Délon king, but I couldn't rule the Délons because I was still human. I was a warrior, but I couldn't fight this fight because it was another warrior's battle. I was tired of not having any power.

I was about to not so calmly explain to Tarak why I would fight this battle, and there was nothing he or the other Keepers could do to stop me, when I felt a tug on my jeans around my knees. I looked down and saw the almond-shaped eyes of Nate looking back at me. I was stunned at first. He was no bigger than a loaf of bread the last time I saw him. Now he was walking, albeit with a great deal of difficulty.

I reached down and picked him up. "Hello, Nate."

He clumsily reached out and tweaked my nose. His mouth was agape in a wondrous grin. Drool hung from his chin.

"Do you remember me?" I asked.

He pressed his lips together and did an uncanny impression of a motorboat. Spit bubbles formed at the corners of his mouth.

R.W. Ridley

"He's a handful, that one," Wes said. "Boy's got all kinds of energy. Takes pert' near all of us to keep him entertained."

"He's so big," I said.

"Big and fussy," Wes replied.

"Good thing there's so many of you..." I stopped in mid sentence. I scanned the eyes of everyone in the room. I saw their faces then, as I remembered them, in my mind's eye. There was something wrong. Something was missing... Not something. Someone.

"Ajax." I said the name with a sense of urgency. Like I was commanding that they bring him to me now.

Wes hesitated. He looked at Tarak for guidance. Tarak simply nodded.

Before they could formulate a nice adult explanation as to where Ajax was, Tyrone spoke up and simply said, "They got him."

"The Délons?" I asked out of reflex more than anything else. I knew it was the Délons.

"Yep," Tyrone answered.

"He put up a hell of a fight," Wes added. "Took six of 'em out before they was able to get a net around him."

"Did they..." I didn't want to know the answer to the question so I stopped. Whether they changed him into a Délon or not didn't matter. I decided I preferred not to know. But Wes read my mind and answered the question I didn't ask.

"He ain't one of them. They got him and the other go-rillas locked up somewhere, prisoners. I hear tell they make 'em fight for sport."

"Where?"

"Délon City," Wes said. "Don't know much beyond that."

I owed Ajax my life. The thought of him as a prisoner forced to fight his own kind for the amusement of the Délons sickened me. "I'm going there tomorrow."

"What in the world of pig snot for?" Wes asked.

I wasn't really sure how to answer the question. I chuckled nervously. "You might want to sit down for this."

Wes did as suggested. "What is it, kid?"

"I don't know exactly how to put this."

"Put it in plain English and just spit it out, boy." Wes folded his arms over his chest. They rested on top of his huge potbelly.

I did as he requested. "I'm their king."

There was a jolt of suffering silence. They all stared at me blankly. Except for Nate. He fidgeted in my arms.

"Whose king?" Tyrone asked.

"The Délons." I said it quickly. Like I was ripping a band-aid off.

"What are you saying?" Valerie asked.

"I'm the Délon king."

They all looked at each other. Tyrone was the first to laugh. The others, including Tarak, quickly joined in.

"What's so funny?" I asked.

"How'd you go and manage something like that?" Wes asked.

"I didn't manage anything. It just happened."

"A human cannot be Délon king," Tarak said.

"I know." I didn't want to be king of the purple freaks, but I was more than a little upset that my friends thought it was so funny that I could be their king. "Look, I didn't ask to be king. It was Roy's idea."

Tarak suddenly stopped laughing. "General Roy?"

"The very same," I said.

"This doesn't make sense." Tarak stood and bumped his head on the ceiling. Chunks of plaster fell to the floor.

Wes didn't appear to know why Tarak was so upset, but he had learned that whenever the big hairy goon got worried, they all should worry. He suddenly forgot why he was laughing. "What's wrong, Fluffy?" He had taken to calling Tarak "Fluffy" mostly because it made Tarak mad.

"General Roy is to be king." Tarak brushed the bits of ceiling from his shoulder. "It is written."

"Looks like they've gone off script," I said. "Because I got marked by the royal scarab and everything."

"Marked?" Tarak's hair stood on end. He stood fully erect and punched a hole through the tiled ceiling with his massive head. He spread his arms out wide and let out an ear-piercing roar. In one swift motion he lurched forward and snatched Nate from my arms, knocking Wes, Tyrone, and Valerie to the ground.

"Hey!" I screamed.

"What's the big idea?" Valerie screeched.

"He's been marked by the royal scarab," Tarak said retreating to the back of the room cradling Nate in his left hand. "It's not safe."

"Wait a minute! Wait..." I was somewhat disoriented from Tarak's sudden outburst. "I... I..." My mind was racing. The lingering doubt I had managed to shake about my own trustworthiness was building momentum in my gut again. I did not want what the Délons wanted. What did Tarak mean 'It's not safe.'

"Now, hold on just a fat feathered minute," Wes said as he struggled to get his portly frame up off the floor. "Oz is Oz, and ain't nothing going to change that. I know it sure as I'm standing here."

"He's been marked." Tarak crouched in the corner seemingly afraid for his life.

"You keep saying that, and it don't make a damn bit of difference to me. Plenty of people have been marked. They's as harmless as someone who ain't." I was heartened by Wes's defense of me.

"People who are marked," Tarak said, the timbre of his voice grew softer and softer as he spoke, "are..." The big white monster searched for the right word. "Open vessels of information."

"You've gone loco, Fluffy." Wes crossed his eyes and twirled his index finger near his ear.

I knew what Tarak meant by open vessels of information. The Délons were monitoring me. I don't know how, but they knew my thoughts... No, that's not exactly right. They knew what I was feeling. It had something to do with the marking. They were tracking my emotions as if they were feeding off them.

"I have to go," I said as I moved toward the back exit.

"What?" Wes followed after me.

"Don't go, man," Tyrone pleaded.

"Don't listen to that big hair ball," Wes said. "Stay."

"It's not safe," I said. I reached Tarak and tried to get him to make eye contact with me. He turned away. I got a last fleeting glimpse of Nate as Tarak covered the toddler completely from my view.

"Tarak," Valerie moaned. "Tell Oz to stay. Tell him you didn't mean it."

"It's okay," I said sounding more abrupt than I intended. "He's right. It's not safe for me to be here." I turned to them with a brave face, but my heart was about to fall out of my chest. I felt at home with them. I felt protected. I didn't want to leave.

"C'mon, kid," Wes said. "Tarak's wrong about this. I know it like I know a chocolate bar is sweet. He ain't nothing but an overgrown poodle with on overactive imagination."

"He's our Keeper, Wes. You need to listen to him." I walked out of the mattress store.

Wes followed. "We gotta come up with a plan, Oz. We set out to bring everybody back. Remember?"

"They are back." I continued to walk away.

"That's a bunch of bull and you know it. Ain't nothing back but a gang of purple things with crazy spider legs on their heads, and purple-about-to-bes. This ain't back. This ain't nowhere near back."

"I can't help you."

"Damn it, boy!" Wes roared. I could feel his anger chasing me down as I turned the corner of the mattress store. "Don't you run away from this. We need you."

Chubby saw me and started to approach. "It's too dangerous, Wes."

"Dangerous?" Wes belly laughed. "Good night and good crap, Oz. It reached about a half past dangerous a great while back. We're staring down the gullet of one of those do or die moments you always hear about."

I mounted Chubs. "You heard Tarak..."

"And Tarak's a fine fella'... or monster... or big ol' shaggy ape, but he ain't right about this. I know that like I know the sky is..."

I smiled. "You were going to say like you know the sky is blue." I smiled through the purple haze of the Délon night. "Like I said before, I'm going to Atlanta... Délon City tomorrow. Me and Lou." Wes's face lit up when he heard Lou's name. "And some others. Can you follow us without being seen?"

"Invisible is my middle name." He smiled.

"We have to find Ajax," I said. "This won't work without him."

"So we're going to do this? We're going to fight?"

"You'll have to convince Tarak."

"That big ball of fur will come around. You'll see."

I turned Chubby toward the road. "Then it's settled. We fight." I tapped chubby in the ribs with my heel, and he trotted back to Tullahoma.

EIGHT

I was saddle weary by the time I got back to the house. I jumped off Chubby's back and hit the ground flat footed. My knees instantly ached and my back throbbed. I shuffled toward the back door.

I had spent most of the ride back from the mattress store in Manchester wiping the tears from my eyes. I had gone there looking for... I don't know exactly what I was looking for. I wanted to feel safe, to feel like I wasn't alone in this. But instead, I felt more alone than ever.

"I wanted what they wanted." I said it to myself over and over again on the road home. I didn't know what Mrs. Dayton meant by it, and I tried to convince myself she couldn't be right. But my encounter with Tarak made me doubt myself even more, and there is no lonelier feeling on earth than when you doubt yourself.

I stepped up to the back door, and took a deep breath. I couldn't let anyone else see the uncertainty in my face, although I was sure they were all asleep. I was a king. I was a warrior. I was a fourteen-year-old kid who had to conquer the world. Doubt was not an option.

I opened the door. The house was dark and alive. A pungent burning sugary odor beat against my face when I moved toward the kitchen. It stung my nostrils.

Gordy was crashed on the floor in the living room and Lou

was stretched out on the couch. Devlin was nowhere around.

I crept along the wooden floor, feeling the stiff boards strain and creek beneath my feet. I sniffed the air trying to find the source of the smell. In the front foyer, I stepped in a puddle of goop, a clear liquefied rubber that stuck to the bottom of my shoe. I bent down to examine it. It wasn't a puddle. It was a trail that wound down the hall toward my parent's room.

The smell grew more intense the closer I got to the room. I tiptoed down the remainder of the hallway, my back against the wall. I knew that once I found the source of the smell I would be sorry I did. "That's a bell you can't unring," my grandfather used to say, but I felt compelled to do it. My curiosity trumped my common sense. I placed my hand on the doorknob to my parents' room and let it linger. I could practically see the odor drifting from underneath the door. As I stood there working up the courage to open the door, I heard a series of high-pitched squeaks and low moans. I tried to convince myself that ignorance was bliss, to just walk away and pretend the odor and the noises didn't exist, but my need to know forced me to turn the knob and step inside the room.

I expected the room to be dark, but it wasn't. It was more than dark. The darkness had been sucked from the room, and all that remained was a thick, soupy blackness. The burnt sugary odor barreled past the doorframe like an avalanche. I stooped with my hands on my knees, and felt my stomach twist in a knot. Within seconds, I vomited violently on my mother's nice wood floors. I rose and wiped my mouth on my sleeve.

The squeaking grew louder and more panicked as I took another step inside the room. I flipped the light switch, and was not surprised when the light did not come on. The light from the hallway poured in and fought through the blackness to illuminate my parents' bed. Slowly, I could make out the figures of Mom and Pop sleeping beneath the covers.

They were both on their backs. I scanned their bodies starting at their feet. The smell circled me. It felt as though it were pecking at my face as I moved closer to the bed. As if it were warning me to stay back. I looked at my parents' faces and swallowed a scream.

Their faces were gone, covered by large purple jellyfish-like masks. The jellyfish monsters pulsated and squeaked. The odor that had lured me into my parents' room wafted from these grotesque little blobs. In an instant, I knew what I was looking at were shunters. They were sucking the humanity from my parents and replacing it with Délon blood.

I ran to my mother's side, and searched my mind for a plan of action. Nothing useful entered my head. I reached out to ply the shunter from her face, but a long whip-like tail appeared out of nowhere and slashed me across the face. I stumbled backwards wiping the blood from my cheek.

I grabbed the lamp off the nightstand and raised it over my head. I lowered my arms when I realized that slamming the lamp down on the shunter wouldn't do my mother's face much good.

I held the lamp out in front of me with one arm to try to block the tail as I reached out with the other arm to remove the shunter from my mother's face. I placed my hand on the slimy blob and the tail whipped towards me again. It caught the lamp repeatedly as it whipped back and forth. I tried to peel the shunter from my mother's face with the other hand.

The purple blob would not let go. I looked closer and could see thousands of tiny tentacles digging into my mother's face and head. Through the shunter's purple gelatin mass, I could see my mother's eyes darting back and forth.

The shunter's tail ripped the lamp from my hand and flung it across the room. With invisible speed, it whipped the tail back toward me and struck me on the ear. I tumbled to the floor.

A low rhythmic laughter came from the back corner of my parents' room. It was Délon laughter. I placed one hand on my throbbing, ringing ear and looked into the deep dark corner, praying that the laughter would soon stop.

"They don't like to be touched." The voice belonged to Devlin.

"You think?" I said sarcastically. I stood. "Call them off."

"They're not dogs, Oz. You can't give them a command, a treat, a pat on the head, and expect them to obey." Devlin's purple face now glowed in the darkness. His white eyes beamed.

"How do I get them off, then?"

"You don't."

"That's crap, and you know it!" I stepped toward him.

"Why would you want to? Look at them. It's a beautiful thing to watch."

"Stop this, now!"

He stood. His spider legs flared. His mouth opened and the insect mandibles snapped. In a motion too quick for me to detect he leapt on top of me and pinned me to the floor. "I should break your neck!"

"Do it and General Roy will make you skinner food." I struggled to breathe with the full weight of Devlin on top of me.

"Mercy!" he screamed.

"What?"

"Explain this mercy to me," he said. "This thing you showed me before... at the school."

"Oh, mercy..." I wheezed. "But you've got to get off me. I can't breathe."

Devlin reluctantly complied and stood up. I crawled backwards with one arm and massaged my bruised chest with the other. I stood with difficulty.

My eyes immediately zeroed in on my parents again. "Mercy

would be to get those things off my parents' faces."

"It would kill them," Devlin said. "Is that mercy?"

I thought long and hard about the question. It may have in fact been the most merciful thing to do, but I wasn't about to give Devlin permission to kill my parents. "No."

"Then what is?"

"Easing someone's suffering."

His face twisted into confusion. "But suffering is so... delicious."

I shuddered. "Not for humans. Suffering is pain. Don't you remember any of this? From before?"

"Before what?" he asked.

"Never mind," I said remembering Délons don't like to be reminded that they were once human. "Humans are about compassion. We treat each other in a way so as not to cause one another harm."

His expressionless white eyes seemed to zero in on me. "We are here because humans were made to suffer by other humans. The Storytellers created our kind because they were tormented by others like you. Is this not true?"

I faltered. "That's not what I mean..." He had me. I didn't know what to say. "Look, we don't always get it right. We humans make a lot of mistakes, but most of us, we try to do the right thing."

"Then mercy is the right thing?"

"Yes, it is. I haven't always shown it, but I'm trying to make up for that now."

"Mercy is a waste of time," Devlin said.

"You'd be dead if weren't for mercy. General Roy was going to kill you."

He tilted his head. His white eyes narrowed. He was churning this last bit of logic over in his twisted gray matter. His face looked pained. I could tell he was being punished by the Délon collective for even considering the concept of mercy. "Enough!" he barked. "We should leave the shunters. They will be finished for the night soon."

"But my parents..."

"Trust me. You don't want to be here when they finish. They will be hungry. And they aren't very choosy about what they eat. Instinct will send them back to their solifipods to feed, but if they should find something along the way..."

I cringed at the thought. "I get the point." I took one last look at my parents before we left. I wanted desperately to help them, but I couldn't. I was growing tired of feeling helpless all the time.

***

I slept lightly for the next couple of hours. I didn't dream. In fact, I hadn't dreamt since this whole thing started. I guess there's no point in it when you're living a nightmare.

I lay in bed most of the time trying to forget what was happening to my parents. It wasn't easy with my own solifipod sitting just a few feet away in the corner of my room. I thought many times about smashing the thing to pieces, but I knew the Délon collective would be on top of me before I sat back down.

Part of me felt it was cowardly to think that way. After all, my parents were dying at the other end of the house and I was lying in bed thinking of ways not to make the Délons mad. A real warrior wouldn't assess the risks. He would act and rely on his instincts to see him through a battle. I wasn't a real warrior. I don't think I even wanted to be one anymore. Fighting was too hard. I was just a kid. I shouldn't have to fight. It wasn't fair to expect me to take on the Délons. It wasn't too long ago that I had trouble matching my socks without my mom's help. Now I was trying to figure out how to save the world. It didn't make sense.

The room to my door slowly opened. I sat up in bed to see Gordy enter. He was yawning and wiping the sleep from his eyes. "Dude, Purple Pete says we've got to move out soon."

"Who?"

"Purple Pete, the big Délon..."

"Devlin."

"Whatever. He went out to get his grub on. He wants us up and ready to go by the time he gets back."

I kicked the covers off and hung my feet over the side of the bed. "The horses here?"

"Yeah, but we're not really riding those things are we?"

I smiled. "You'll get used to it."

"What's wrong with taking a van or something. Hell, you're the king. Let's take a Hummer."

"I'm not the king." I stood and stretched. "Besides Délons don't ride in cars... apparently."

"That's so weird."

"That's weird? Have you looked outside lately, Gordy? This whole world's weird."

"You know what I mean." He walked over to my desk and grabbed my regulation size NFL football. Without looking at me he said, "How bad you think it hurts?"

"What?"

"The change... you know..."

Unfortunately, I did know. I thought about my parents. Watching those shunters digging into their skulls and doing whatever they do did not look like a trip to an amusement park. "A lot."

"Not to sound like a real Nancy-boy, but I'd pay a million

dollars if I could get out of that."

"You and me both." A thought suddenly came to me. "Where's your solifipod?"

"My what?"

"Your solifipod." I pointed to the corner of the room where my solifipod was breathing in and out.

"I don't have one."

I grabbed the football out his hand. He was lying to me. *Beware of G,* popped into my head. "Bull. You got marked. You told me yourself."

"So."

"If you get marked, you get one of those little bug-in-a-bag thingies as a nice little door price." I was trying to remain calm, but my distrust for Gordy was growing by the second.

"Fine then," he said. "It's at my house."

"Show me." I scrambled to find my shoes.

"Show you? We don't have time to walk over to my house and get back here before grumpy Purple Pete comes back from breakfast." He was looking nervous, and that didn't make me happy.

"We'll take the horses. Lou can stall Devlin if he gets back before us." One shoe on, I slipped my foot into the other. "Let's go." I grabbed Gordy by the arm and led him out of the room.

"This is crazy," he said. "Let's just leave it."

"This isn't about taking it with us. This is about proving you have one."

"You don't believe me?" Gordy said sounding genuinely hurt.

Lou watched in wide-eyed wonder as I practically dragged Gordy out of my room. "What's going on?"

Gordy shook loose of my grip. "I've got one, you dink. I'm not lying."

"Yeah, well you're going to have to prove it."

Délon City

"I thought we were friends," he shouted.

"Not anymore," I shouted back. "Not here, not in this world. This is a whole new ball game. I don't know who is who or what is what. If we make this trip to Atlanta or Délon City or whatever you want to call it, the Délons are going to expect those of us who've been marked to bring their solifipods with them. Am I right, Lou?"

"You're right," she said.

"What about her?" Gordy snapped. "Aren't you going to ask where her solif... a-thing is?"

I looked at her. It had never occurred to me to ask her before. She had been a prisoner of General Roy and Reya for months now. Surely they would have marked her.

"I haven't been marked," she said. "The general has special plans for me."

I hesitated because I didn't know if I believed her. I didn't know if I believed anybody. I quickly turned my attention back to Gordy. "Let's go."

"But I can't ride a horse. I don't know how."

"I'll show you." I grabbed him and shoved him towards the door.

"Okay, okay, but I'm telling you right now, I'm not taking that little creepy thing with me."

"You'll do what I say," I said as I pushed him out the door. I turned back to Lou. I scanned her face to see if I could see any eye twitches or irregular breathing. Anything to let me know she was lying. Nothing. "We'll be back."

***

The ride to Gordy's house was just a few miles, but Gordy's lack of riding skills made the trip slow and long. He sat in the saddle like there were thorns on it, and he seemed to be hyperventilating the entire time he was on the horse's back.

I dismounted Chubby as soon as we arrived at Gordy's house. Despite Gordy's obvious dislike for his horse, he didn't dismount right away. He stared at the house as if it would swoop down and gobble him up. As I watched him slowly and clumsily swing his right leg over the saddle and slide off his horse's back, I got the feeling he hadn't been to his house in days, maybe weeks.

He stood next to his horse and glared at his house. Tears welled up in his eyes. I suddenly felt like the world's biggest jerk for forcing him to come back here. We should have gotten back on the horses and ridden away as fast as we could. If I had the chance to do it over again a thousand times, that's exactly what I would do every time given what I know now about what was in that house.

I started walking toward the front door.

"No," Gordy said with a sense of urgency. "It's in the garage." He stepped away from the horse and breathed deeply.

I motioned for him to move ahead of me so that I could follow. He complied with a great deal of reluctance. It was as if I were marching him down the corridor of an old prison to the electric chair. He was ghost white and shaking all over.

"I'll show you this silly-pod thing and then we're out of here, okay?" he said.

"Sure, sure," I answered.

He kept an eye on the front door as he lead me to the garage. He walked as if he could be attacked from any direction at any moment. His head was on a swivel.

A thought came to me. "Where's your dad?"

"The creep's in Délon City with the rest of the purple whack pack."

"Do all the Délons live in Délon City?"

Délon City

"Only the good ones, and by good I mean big, bad, and ugly."
We reached the corner of the garage and moved to the side door.
Gordy put his hand on the knob. "Remember, I prove this thing's
here and we leave."

I nodded.

He pushed the door open and stepped inside. A stale, humid
wind exited the garage as we entered. It was a dark and musty
expanse inside. One car sat in the two-car garage like a slumbering
beast. The rest of the space was an oddly organized mishmash
of neatly stacked boxes and erratic heaps of household items.

In the corner of the room was a huge chest-high white freezer.
Gordy's old man used it to store venison after his hunting trips.
It looked like an industrial-sized coffin. It let out a low hum. If I
had just arrived here from another planet, I would have thought it
was alive.

Gordy pointed at the freezer. "It's in there."

"Open it," I said.

"Not me," Gordy said backing away. "You want to see it so
bad, you open it."

I took a step toward the freezer, and then reconsidered. "I
think you should do it."

"I don't think either of us should do it," he said.

"It's your solifipod."

"You can have it." He laughed nervously.

"I'm king, remember."

"Suddenly you want to be king?" he asked.

"I... I..."

He cut me off. "I-I nothing. It was your idea to come over
here and find this thing. You should be the one who opens the
freezer. Since we're not friends anymore, you can suck on a rotten
egg for all I care."

"I didn't mean we're not friends anymore exactly..."

"Whatever. All I know is that freezer ain't going to open itself." He crossed his arms and raised an eyebrow. "This is your party."

I shook my head and sighed. He was right. I walked to the freezer, placed my hand on the recessed handle on the top and stopped. I couldn't bring myself to do it. I turned and searched the garage for a weapon. I spotted a tool chest on the opposite side of the garage and ran to it. Inside was a hammer. I retrieved it and returned to the freezer. Gordy watched me with baffled wonderment the whole time.

I counted to three and ripped opened the freezer. Cold air escaped and then sucked back into the frozen enclosure. My hammer raised in one hand, I reached inside with the other and searched through the icy fog for the solifipod. My hand skimmed across dozens of packs of deer meat before I found it. It was frozen and lifeless. The cold fog lifted, and I could finally see it. It was dead.

"Did you find it?" Gordy asked, still standing in his original spot.

"Yeah," I said.

"Well?"

"I don't understand. These things are tuned into the Délon collective. You should be dead."

"It's the cold," he said.

"What?"

"My old man let it slip when he was going through the change. Délons don't last long in the cold because they get cut off from the collective. Which is weird because when I went through my marking I didn't feel nothing but cold."

"Me, too," I said.

"So, that's it, right? We can leave?"

"Yeah, we can leave..." A crash came from above our heads.

Délon City

"What was that?"

"Nothing, man. Let's just go." Gordy bolted for the door.

The crash came again, and I heard a muffled cry.

"There's somebody in your house, Gordy."

"No there ain't. Come on."

A voice shot through the walls. "Gordy?"

Gordy turned sickly white.

"Gordy?" the voice cried again.

"Who is that?" I asked.

But Gordy didn't answer. He fell to his knees and began to weep.

"What's going on, Gordy?"

"It's my sister!" he shouted. "It's my sister, all right. You happy? It's my stinking little sister!"

"I thought you said the Délons fed her to the skinners?"

She cried out again. "Gordy?"

"I told you we shouldn't have come here," he said. "I told you." He wiped the snot from his nose.

"You said..."

"I said they fed her to the skinners," he shouted. "And they did."

Another crash from overhead.

"But they didn't let them finish," Gordy continued.

"What are you saying?" I kept my eyes on the garage ceiling.

"I'm saying the Délons are dirty filthy pigs who get their sick kicks all kinds of ways. They let the skinners do what they do until sis didn't have a shred of skin, and then they killed the little stick bugs."

My mouth dropped open. I couldn't believe what he was saying. "You mean..."

"She lived for a couple of days. I tried to take care of her, but what do I know? She died because she couldn't take the pain anymore."

I looked at him confused. "She died? But she's not dead."

"There's all kinds of dead in the Délons' world." He stood. His sister shouted in anger this time. "Gordy, come here!"

"What kind of dead is that?" I asked.

"You don't want to know, Oz. You don't want to know."

"Please, Gordy," his sister begged this time.

"We have to help her," I said.

"Trust me. There ain't nothing to help. That ain't my sister." He quickly moved to the door to leave the garage.

"I'm going up," I said.

"No," he barked. "Not a chance. I won't let you do it. It's my sister. Just leave it alone."

"You just said that wasn't your sister." I walked past the car and opened the door to the house.

"Dude, don't do this. I'm telling you... I'm not coming with you," He said.

"Fine," I said. "Go wait by the horses."

"If you go up there, I won't have nothing to wait for. She's skinner dead."

I turned to him. "What's that mean?"

"That means she ain't nothing but a walkin', talkin', skinless skinner. She's got one thing on her mind."

"What's that?"

"Eating," he said. He gave me one last look and then exited the garage.

That should have been enough for me to turn back, but it wasn't. Something deep inside of me drove me to walk through the door and stand in the dark kitchen of Gordy's house.

NINE

I stood in the kitchen for what seemed an eternity. All the while I could hear Gordy's sister begging for help upstairs. I gripped and re-gripped the handle of the hammer 50 or so times as I worked up the courage to make the first step toward the stairs. The longer I hesitated the more it seemed like a bad idea. Then something unexpected happened. Gordy's sister called out my name.

"Oz Griffin. I smell Oz Griffin." She cackled and then wept. "Help me, Oz Griffin."

I swallowed the lump in my throat and stepped toward the hallway leading to the stairs. My heart was fluttering like a nervous butterfly. As I got closer to the stairs, I asked myself one question. "What the hell are you doing, Oz?"

I had no acceptable answer, but still I pushed forward. I took the stairs one step at a time, stopping to reassess what I was doing every step of the way. I gripped the hammer with both hands now. My breathing was labored.

I reached the top of the stairs and made myself as flat as I could against the wall. I scanned both ends of the hallway.

"Someone's upstairs," Gordy's sister called out. "And someone smells so good... so tasty..."

That was all I needed to hear. I bolted back down the stairs. Halfway down, I heard a deafening screaming. "Oz, help me!

Don't let them get me!"

I stopped. It was a trap. My mind knew it. But it was Gordy's sister. If there was the smallest chance she could be helped, then I had to help her. I walked back up the stairs as if I were climbing the final peak on Everest. Every step was carefully calculated, and every prayer I had ever heard in my life came spewing out of my mouth uncontrollably.

I stood in the upstairs hallway, eyes focused on the room above the garage. I flipped the light switch, but nothing came on.

"No lights. No eyelids. No lights. No eyelids." The voice screeched throughout the house.

I moved down the hallway as silently as I could, but still she heard me. She counted each step I took. "Three steps closer. Four steps closer. Here he comes. Here he comes!"

"Allie," I said.

"He calls me Allie!" Her voice was shrill with excitement. "Allie Flynn."

"Ten steps closer. Eleven steps closer. Twelve steps and at the door. He's at the door! He's at the door!"

"Allie," I said. "You're not making this easy. I want to help you."

"Help me, Oz Griffin. Please, help me."

I turned the knob and let the door open slowly on its own. The room was a guest bedroom. The mattress from the bed was stacked against the window to keep out the light. *No lights. No eyelids.* She had said.

In the darkest corner of the room, directly opposite the door, I saw a silhouette of a little girl. She stood motionless. She was taller than I remember.

"We're so hungry, Oz Griffin."

I forced myself to move forward. The hammer was raised, cocked back, and ready to crash down on her head at any time.

110

Délon City

"Take it easy, Allie. I'm here to help."

Two-thirds of the way to Allie, I realized it wasn't her at all. It was a coat rack. I stood in the middle of the room, completely vulnerable. I scanned the room in every direction. My heart went from a nervous flutter to a brutal pounding. "Allie?"

"We're so hungry."

The voice came from above me. I jerked my head up. There, crawling on the ceiling like an insect, was Gordy's little sister. Her skinless body was fire red with patches of black. She wore a lipless grin.

"Can't you see how hungry we are?" she cried.

"We?"

Slowly dozens of skinners emerged from underneath her, their razor-like mandibles rubbing together.

I attempted to back away, but tripped over the naked bed frame. Skinners started to rain from the ceiling. Allie leapt from the ceiling and landed on my chest.

"Thank you for bringing us food," she said. Her lidless eyes bulged. Saliva dripped from her mouth as she chomped her teeth. I could feel the skinners starting to take little bites.

"Get off!" I screamed. "Gordy, help!"

A beam of light shot across the room, and struck Allie in the face. She screeched and leapt out of its path. The skinners were still nibbling away. I stood, shaking and swatting at the bugs.

"Leave!" a voice commanded. It was Délon Devlin standing in the doorway with a flashlight. I was never so glad to see a Délon.

"How..."

"Leave before the skinners eat my king."

"No light. No eyelids!" Gordy's sister screamed.

I rushed to the door. "What about her?"

He smiled. "Don't worry, I will show her mercy." He stepped

111

back and let me pass. "And I will have fun doing so."

I turned back and watched as Allie deftly climbed up the wall and on the ceiling. "Don't let the tasty boy go," she whined. "We are so hungry."

I raced down the hallway, and down the stairs as Devlin started to put Allie out her misery.

***

Lou and Devlin were waiting on horseback when I emerged from the house. The expression on my face must have told them everything they needed to know, because they didn't ask a single question. I simply walked over to Chubby, climbed on his back, and waited in silence for Devlin to finish his business.

I was disheartened to see my backpack with my solifipod hanging on the saddle horn of my horse. It wriggled and twisted. Chubby seemed uneasy, so I snatched it up and looped my arms through the straps before I had time to think about it. If I had taken the time to think about it, I probably would have smashed it on the ground and had Chubby stomp on it.

We waited only about five minutes before Devlin exited the house with a grotesque Délon smile. He had clearly enjoyed putting Allie out of her misery. I hated him and appreciated him all at once. I guess that's how most people feel about the devils in their lives.

He leapt on his horse's back and gave the command to move. And we did, like a sad, sulking caravan of pre-schoolers off to see a circus we had no interest in seeing.

We passed various residents of Tullahoma as we rode through the town. Some were human, some were going through the change, and some were halfers. All of them looked at us as if we were part of a presidential procession. It was strange and

Délon City

unsettling.

As we entered Manchester, I noticed there was very little traffic. There were only a few cars here and there. Had this been normal times, there would have been a steady stream of cars going back and forth from Tullahoma to Manchester.

I was on the constant lookout for Wes's van. I peeked over my shoulder so often Devlin started to get suspicious. I reined it in and kept my nervous anticipation in check as best I could.

On top of Monteagle, the temperature was cold enough that a dusting of snow stuck to the ground. The humans on horseback bundled up in two or three layers and we all pulled skullcaps over our ears. Devlin was cold, but he never covered up his shredded Délon uniform. He seemed disoriented at times, and I could swear he shrunk about an inch and a half while we were on top of the mountain.

Given the Délons' troubles with the cold, I was surprised that they still "allowed" cold weather. After all, this was their world created by their Storyteller, shouldn't they have control over everything, including the elements? That's when it occurred to me. The Délons didn't have control over their own world. They were in fact as helpless as humans were in our world. Even though they controlled their own Storyteller, they were at the mercy of fate.

I smiled as I realized this because it meant one thing. The Délons could be beat.

***

We traveled the same route we did when the Takers were the monsters of choice. As we passed South Pittsburg, I couldn't help but think about our first encounter with the bicycle gang. Roy stayed in the shadows, while Reya and the others tried to

113

steal our horses. They would have, too, if it hadn't been for Ajax. He was definitely the kind of ape you wanted to have on your side.

I couldn't believe I was thinking it, but I missed those days. There was something simple about our mission then. We knew what had to do, and we did it. Not like now.

I still wanted my home back, but defeating the Délons would not get me there. I knew that now. There was something much bigger at play that I had to figure out. Making the Délons go away would only clear the way for the next Storyteller's monsters.

Dr. Hollis, Pepper Sand's shrink, knew about the treatment that Stevie Dayton went through. He had called it Hyper Mental Imaging. Individuals with Down syndrome were taught to cope with their condition by visualizing. Only some of them were too good at it. Some of them learned to do more than visualize. They learned to make things happen with their minds. They learned to bring the monsters they created on paper to life to deal with the monsters in their real lives. Now, the lines were blurred.

We deserved it. Those of us who treated Stevie and others with this condition like retards, we deserved being on the business end of the abuse we dished out. I didn't blame Stevie for where I was. I blamed myself. And nobody with half a brain would disagree with me. When you daydream and create an elaborate fantasy that positions you as the hero and the world around you in desperate need of your super heroic talents, you never imagine that the evil you are battling is really of your own creation as well. But it is. It's your mind, your fantasy, your evil.

I looked at Lou riding ahead of me. The first time I saw her, she looked like a ratty little homeless kid. Now, she was downright pretty. I didn't want to think of her that way, but I couldn't help myself.

What had she done to deserve this nightmare? I knew why

Gordy was here. He was a bigger jerk than me, but Lou didn't strike me as the type to pick on the less fortunate. On the contrary, she seemed like the type who would give one of her kidneys to the less fortunate. Yet here she was, riding alongside me, trying to survive this hell. Why?

I tapped Chubby in the ribs with my heels and rode alongside her. "We haven't had much time to talk," I said.

She smiled. "I guess we've been kind of busy."

Riding next to her, I found myself thinking she wasn't just pretty. She was beautiful. What the hell was happening to me? Lou was a warrior. I couldn't think of her that way. "Funny, now that we have the time, I don't know what to talk about?"

"Yeah," she said. "I know what you mean. There's not much use for small talk in this world. Seems kind of silly and pointless."

"That's what small talk is," I said. "But I know what you mean."

We rode in uncomfortable silence for a few excruciating moments. She cleared her throat and spoke up. "I heard about your parents... What you saw, I mean."

"Yeah," I replied. I found myself hoping against hope that we could find a way to stick to small talk.

"They won't remember it, you know."

I looked at her and tried to decide if that mattered.

"It's like being born. Nobody remembers being born."

"I guess so," I said. "But..." I didn't want to have this conversation, but I couldn't help it. My mouth shot off before my mind had time to shut it down. "I saw my Mom's face... She was in pain."

I saw a thousand lies run through Lou's head. She wanted to tell me that my Mom wasn't in pain. She wanted to tell me that everything was going to be all right. She wanted to tell me that I would get over what I saw happening to my parents, but thankfully she didn't. I would have lost all respect for her if she had. She leaned in and whispered, "Use it."

"What?"

She looked to see how far ahead Devlin was. He was out of earshot. "Make them pay, Oz. Make those purple rats eat dirt and die."

I smiled. That was the Lou I knew. "Yeah, I'm working on it."

"If we find their Source before they do, this whole thing is over."

I shook my head. "We've got to be smart about this. Look where killing the Taker Queen got us."

"Nothing could be worse than this," she said.

"We don't know that."

"You don't know, Oz. You haven't seen the things I've seen. You think what's happening to your parents is bad. It's nothing compared to 90% of the stuff I've seen Roy and Reya do. If they find the Source before us, it's only going to get worse."

I looked over my shoulder. "Well, whatever we do, we're going to need more than me, you, and Gordy."

Lou looked in the direction I was looking. "They're about two miles behind us."

"Who?" I asked.

"The 'more' you're talking about. Wes, Tyrone, Valerie... probably some others I couldn't see." She smiled

"How did..."

"They parked in front of your house after you and Gordy left this morning. They've been following us the whole time."

I motioned toward Devlin. "Does he know?"

She shook her head. "I don't think so. If it doesn't involve food, Devlin doesn't pay attention."

I laughed. "Some things never change."

Délon City

Lou laughed with me.

Devlin turned to see what was so funny. "Stop your cackling," he screeched. He turned back around.

Lou and I stifled our laughs. We both found it strange that we could find something to laugh at, but we welcomed it nonetheless.

Gordy awkwardly trotted up next to us. "What gives with you two?"

We didn't answer.

"How long are we going to ride? My back is killing me. My ribs are sore. My ass feels like someone took a belt to it, and my thighs..."

"All right," I said. "We get the point, Gordy."

"Yeah, well, planes work you know. We could've flown to Délon City. That would have been nice. You're the king. I bet they would have let us sit in first class."

"We're riding horses. Deal with it," I said.

"Can't we at least take a break or something? It's going to be dark soon." As irritating as he was, he was right. It probably was time to stop.

"Devlin," I shouted. "I think the horses need to rest!"

He didn't answer.

"Devlin, we should stop!"

Still no answer.

"Devlin..."

"The horses are fine," he growled. "Shut up and ride."

I gave Chubby a kick and rode up beside Devlin. "We're stopping."

"I said the horses are fine..."

"Well, we're not, and I say we're stopping."

His dead eyes narrowed, and he grabbed me by the collar. "I'm growing exceedingly tired of you, human."

R.W. Ridley

It was my first real look at him since we passed over the mountain. He wasn't the same. There was a weakness to him that I hadn't seen before. He was more tired than any of us. He just didn't know how to deal with it.

"You don't like the cold, do you?" I said.

His grip loosened. His expression turned from anger to confusion. "Who is the man in the white coat?"

Now I was confused. "What?

"The white coat. Who is he, and why is he looking at me?" Devlin nodded toward the exit ahead. There, sitting in a thick leather chair, sat a man in a white coat busily jotting down notes on a pad of paper.

"What the..." I said.

TEN

"What are you doing here?" I ask the man in the white coat.

"I'm not," he smiles. "You're in my office."

I look around. The horses are gone. Lou is gone. Gordy and Devlin are gone. I am in a room lying on a couch. A clinical air swirls around me. My hands. They are not my hands

"What are you doing?" I ask. "I have to go back."

"Oz," the man says. "This isn't healthy. There's no therapeutic benefit to these hypnosis sessions. You're simply reliving events that never happened. Events you've fabricated in your mind."

I'm angry. "Send me back."

He narrows his eyes. "In my opinion it's doing more harm than good."

I stand. Everything inside of me wants to take a swing at him, but I know I can't. He'll never send me back if I do. I breathe deeply. "Look, I know it's not real, but..." I stop to see if he's buying it. "But I have to see this thing through."

"I'm sorry." He says. "I'm afraid I've already let it go too far." His eye twitches. He stands and turns to leave. He stops. Without turning he says, "One thing."

"What?"

"The Source. What is it?"

"What?" I find this to be an odd question. Why does he care

R.W. Ridley

if it's just fantasy.

"The Délon Source. You said the way to defeat the Délons was to find their Source before they did. Obviously you found it. I mean suppose your story isn't fantasy. Suppose everything you've said while you've been under is true. The simple fact that the world is now Délon free means you found the Source. What is it?" He finally turns to me.

"What difference does it make? You don't believe any of it?"

"True," he says sitting back down. "But I do believe the Délons' Source, real or imagined, is the source for your psychosis. Perhaps if you tell me what it was, we can find a more effective treatment for you."

I cock my head to the side and snicker. "You want to know, you're going to have to put me back under."

He laces his fingers together over his belly and sighs. A sound like a metronome suddenly becomes pronounced in the room. The man in the white coat seems to be thinking in time to the rhythmic ticking. He purses his lips and twiddles his fingers.

"Perhaps it does have therapeutic value," he says. "Lie back down."

I comply.

ELEVEN

We stopped at an empty house on I-75, just outside of Chattanooga. The house wasn't just empty. It was abandoned. Once the owners had become Délons, they couldn't bear the thought of living among humans so they made their way south to Délon City.

They left without a care for their former lives. Knowing Délons the way I did at that point, it shouldn't have surprised me, but I couldn't help but wonder how anyone could leave behind old family photos, videos of landmark events in their lives, heirlooms that they probably fought other family members over. It was sickening how disposable their past became to them.

I found a corner in the living room where I could sit and veg out. I was tired. A spent solifipod sat in the opposite corner of the room. Its shunter, having completed its job of turning a human to a Délon, was a dried up carcass curled up inside.

My mind shifted back to Gordy's house. His solifipod was dead. The frigid temperatures of the freezer had killed it. Not just killed it, but cut it off undetected from the Délon collective. Under normal conditions they would have known. They would have felt it, and Gordy would have been skinner food. If that was true, I was beginning to understand General Roy's urgency in finding the Source. They wanted it before the cold weather set in. If the temperatures dropped below freezing in Délon City, all the

Délons would be cut off from each other. They would be alone and vulnerable, easy to defeat. If they had their Source, they may be able to prevent the temperature from dropping.

Don't Trust G... That's what Mrs. Dayton had written. Don't trust Gordy. Why would he have shown me a way to defeat the Délons if he wasn't to be trusted? I had to consider the possibility that I was being set up. That Gordy was purposely leading me down a stray path. To what end, I didn't know, but I had to at least consider the possibility.

A family photo hanging crooked on the wall made me think of my parents. The last time I saw them, shunters were attached to their faces sucking their humanity out. I was instantly struck by feelings of guilt for leaving them behind, for not trying to do more. A warrior would have helped them. A warrior would have died for them.

"You will," a voice said.

I stood. Where had the voice come from? The room spun, and I was suddenly in the warehouse again where I had killed Lou and watched a strange half-crab half-man creature kill Gordy.

"Who said that? Where am I?" The room tilted and vibrated. It was as if it was having trouble sustaining itself. It reminded me of when Délons took on their human appearance. Their faces twitched and bulged. They had trouble hiding their true selves. The same thing was happening with this time jump. It was having trouble existing because it was existing at the wrong time.

The half-crab half-man creature walked out of the darkness on its four spiked legs, its upside down face cocked to the right. It wore a chain around its neck. A slimy tongue dangled from the end of the chain. A souvenir or snack for later, although I couldn't image how it ate with its mouth sewn shut.

It spoke without moving its lips. "They call me Canter."

I readied myself for an attack by the ugly bucket of crust. It was more than twice my size, so I couldn't put up much of a fight against it without a weapon, but I readied myself nonetheless.

"What do you want with me?" I said

"I want you dead."

I backed away.

"But not until you've completed your job."

"Job?"

"Getting rid of those ugly Délons. They are so abhorrent. Don't you think?" It crab-walked to the left.

"You want the Délons dead?"

"Of course," it said. "Why wouldn't I? Their tongues taste awful, and they're hoarding all the humans for themselves."

"But I'm the wrong warrior..."

The crab thing laughed. "It's so cute that you call yourself that. Warrior? How many barely teenage warriors do you know? You're not a warrior. You only stopped wetting your bed a few years ago."

"Eight," I shouted.

"It doesn't make a difference. The other so-called warrior, the one created to kill the Délons, has been captured."

A loud banging came from the other end of the warehouse.

"Here already?" Canter turned and backed away on his spiked crab legs. "No time to talk. We've got to kill your friends."

I looked down and I was holding my sword, J.J. Had I always been holding it? Where did it come from? "What's going on?"

"Boy, you really are dense aren't you? We're going to kill your friends. I'll take the fat, spongy haired kid. You get the girl."

Gordy and Lou walked out of the shadows and started to approach.

"What? Why?"

"Well," Canter groaned. "We're killing the fat kid because he annoys me, and Lou... well, we're killing her because she's a girl."

With that the room shuddered violently and, with no sound at all, the walls of the warehouse exploded. I was back in the house in Chattanooga sitting in the dark quiet corner of the room I had chosen for its solitude. Clearly, solitude wasn't to be had in this world.

We're killing her because she's a girl. What did Canter mean by that? What does being a girl have to do with anything? I sat back down in my chair and tried not to think about what had just happened. All these cryptic messages were driving me crazy. *Don't Trust G... Because she's a girl.* My heart skidded to a stop. I didn't want to say it out loud, but my lips formed the words. "Don't trust girl."

TWELVE

"**Y**ou look lost."

It was Gordy's voice, but it was distant, and hollow. I had slept away from the others. The house was a large two-story traditional southern home with a wraparound porch on both floors. I'd found a spot on the deck off the master bedroom that was shielded from the wind. I'd stayed perfectly warm bundled up in a thick quilted comforter. Now I sat in a cushioned lounge chair and stared out into the moonless purple night wondering how Lou could betray me. I was deep in miserable thought when Gordy found me just before daybreak.

"You look lost," he repeated.

I acknowledged him with a terse nod.

"You mind if I sit?" His hands were buried deep in his pockets. He motioned with his head toward the other lounge chair.

I gave a simple and less terse nod.

He sat, shivering from the cold. "You okay, boss?"

"Boss?"

"Yeah, you're the boss, ain't ya'?"

I thought about the question. "I don't know what I am. I'm not sure what any of us are."

Gordy shook his head. "Don't get deep on me, Oz. I just asked if you're okay."

"Are you okay, Gordy?" I snapped. "Do you get what's going

on here? We're the stars in some cosmic freak show full of monsters that suck the life out of you, and friends who stab you in the back!"

He sat up in his chair and looked at me concerned. "I ain't stabbed no one in the back. I swear to god above I'm on your side..."

"Not you," I shouted. "Not you, okay."

He settled back into his lounger. "Forgive me for assuming it was me. There ain't much else to choose from..." He looked at me in complete shock. "You ain't saying..."

"I don't know what I'm saying," I said. "Forget I said anything."

He looked at me tempted to keep on the topic, but he slowly let it go. His eyes drifted upward. The sky above us wasn't ours, but it was beautiful in its own way. We tried not to admire it, but we couldn't help ourselves. Gordy cleared his throat. "I sure would like to take in a Titans game. I mean the real thing. Not this crazy crap they got going on now."

"Yeah," I said. "That would be cool. The play-off picture would be starting to come together right about now."

"Too bad we got the Colts in our division," he said. "That's usually two losses right there. That only gives us room to lose two or three other games a year."

"What are you talking about?" I asked incredulously. "Two losses? The Colts can be had."

"Please, with that offense, and the way the defense has been playing the last couple of years."

"All you need is a pressure defense..."

And so we talked about a football season that would never be, played by teams that didn't exist anymore, working out probable and improbable playoff scenarios, until pretty soon, we were both sitting in my living room watching the Super Bowl on my family's modest 32-inch TV screen. The Titans had made it of course. Our quarterback position was the excitement of the league. The draft had yielded incredible talent on both sides of the ball. They weren't supposed to be there. Not one so-called football expert picked them to make it, and now that they were in the big game, they were expected to lose badly. They were playing the Cowboys, and nobody but the Steelers beats the Cowboys in the Super Bowl. (That proclamation had been made by an obnoxious Steelers fan calling into our fictitious sports-talk radio show.) This Super Bowl of ours went on until the purple sun was over the tree line in the back of the house.

We had talked the strangeness out of our situation; brought ourselves home for a fleeting moment. It didn't seem like much at the time, but when it was over, when we were forced to get up off the lounge chairs and head downstairs to saddle up the horses, it was the most important conversation we had ever had. Not because it was about football, but because it was about who we used to be, kids. Both of us had forgotten that.

***

Avoiding someone in a four-person caravan on horseback is pretty hard to do. I didn't want to look at Lou, much less speak to her. But I had nowhere to hide from her. She didn't seem to be aware of my attempt to shun her. She would start up various conversations with me, and wasn't concerned by my one-word replies. The more she talked the less I believed Canter. She would never betray me. We had been through too much together.

Still, she had spent a lot of time with Roy and Reya, and she looked no worse for the wear. In fact, she looked better than I had ever seen her. I can't image that the general and his Délon sister were very hospitable hosts. Why hadn't they turned her into a Délon?

"Wait a minute," I whispered to myself. I turned and looked at Lou carefully. Maybe she was a Délon. Maybe she was just wearing her human mask. *Look for twitching. Look to see if the eyes bulge,* I told myself.

Lou caught me looking at her. She smiled. I turned away quickly.

That had to be the answer. She was hiding her Délon appearance behind a human disguise. The other Délons I had seen couldn't sustain the mask for very long, but Lou must have found a way to control it. She was a warrior after all, one of the best I had ever seen. If any Délon could figure out how to sustain the mask, she could.

They were setting me up. Lou would win my confidence without resistance, and I would lead her to the Source. For the moment, I was glad I didn't know what the Source was.

We were midway between Chattanooga and Dalton when I had figured out the Délons' brilliant plan. I barely had time to pat myself on the back when I saw the carcass of a dead deer on the side of the road. At first glance it looked like road kill. Traffic had been light up and down the interstate, but still these things happened.

But as I got closer, I grew more apprehensive. Something about it bothered me. I wasn't sure what it was, but I was growing more and more nervous by the minute. I kicked Chubby and galloped beside Devlin. He looked far from nervous. In fact, he looked giddy.

"What are you so happy about?"

He pointed at the carcass. "Dacs."

"Dacs?"

Gordy let out a sound that was somewhere between a squeak and a bark. "Dacs. Oh man, I thought that was just some crap the kids at school made up."

"They're real," Devlin cackled. "And they're near."

"Anyone want to tell me what a Dac is," I said

"A kind of halfer," Lou answered.

"Not halfer," Devlin snapped. "They're mistakes. Things that never should have been."

"I thought that's what Délons were," I said knowing that it would piss Devlin off.

Devlin was too preoccupied to be pissed off. "Shunters don't always find the right host. They're stupid little jellyfish when you get down to it. They'll attach themselves to whatever's available when they can't find the marked. They'll kill most things they attach themselves to, but every once in a while..." The spider legs on his head flared. "Something will survive."

"Things, what things?" I asked.

"You name it, trees, dogs, cats..."

"Are you trying to tell me that a bunch of half-trees, half Délons killed that deer?" I said.

"Nope," Devlin said calmly, "that would be silly." He dismounted and readied himself for battle. "Most of the Dacs I've seen have been pigs turned Délon, a few dogs. Every once in a while, you see a few exotic animals thrown in, bears, apes."

"Apes?"

"They're the worst," Devlin said, pulling a long metal blade with a cuff attachment from his saddlebag. He hooked it securely to his right arm. "They'll be on us soon. Dismount!" His voice was both angry and excited. He was looking forward to this showdown.

"Shouldn't we keep on riding?" I asked.

"Yeah," Gordy said. "Let's keep riding."

"We fight," Devlin roared. The insect mandibles shot out of his mouth and snapped feverishly.

Gordy turned ghost white. "Can we vote?"

"This is stupid, Devlin. We have no idea how many of these Dacs there are," I said. I realized I was trying the impossible, reasoning with a Délon.

He growled. "You were a great warrior once, or so the legend goes."

Lou interjected. "It's not just a legend. It's true. I was there, and so were you."

I gave her a disapproving glare. I didn't want her defending me. She was a traitor.

Devlin rushed her horse. "I was not there. I was born after the battle of Atlanta..."

"You know what?" I shouted. "I don't care who was where when. Let's concentrate on the present. We got a bunch of these Dacs things headed our way and I say we get on our horses and ride as fast and furious as we can..." Suddenly, I was knocked from my horse. I hit the ground with a heavy thud. The wind was pushed out of my lungs, and I couldn't breathe. A large mass I had not yet identified was on top of me squealing and grunting.

In an instant, my attacker was lifted off me by Devlin. I struggled to catch my breath. I heard the sound a blade of striking flesh over and over again, then a body falling to the ground. When I was able to breathe again, I noticed Lou stooped beside me. She attempted to help me up, but I shrugged her off and stood on my own. I could feel how hurt she was by my refusal of her help.

The thing that attacked me was lying in the middle of the road. Purple streams of blood poured from several stab wounds. It was my first time seeing a Dac. They were uglier than Délons, and I hadn't thought that was possible. This one used to be a pig. Its snot-laden snout was the only way I could tell. It had the tell-tale spider legs and purple skin of a Délon, but the insect mandible hidden inside a Délon's mouth was exposed on this creature. Its entire jaw was more insect than anything else. Its body was man-like in that it had two arms and two legs instead of four legs. The hands and feet were pig's feet. Its build was short and stout.

"Okay," Gordy said. "We've all seen the Dac now. Purple Pete here killed it. Can we leave? I mean really this is... Hey!" His horse raised up on its back legs without warning. The steed's front legs kicked, and he whinnied nervously. Gordy hugged the horse's neck and screamed

Three Dacs approached. Two were pig Dacs like the one Devlin killed, but the third one looked like it used to be a dog. It was hard to tell because it had no fur. Its face was covered with spider legs and large insect mandibles. The only thing that looked remotely like a dog, were the floppy ears on either side of its head. Again, its body was man-like, but its hands and feet remained animal-like. In this case, paws.

The dog Dac leapt on Gordy's horse and wrapped its arm around Gordy's neck. "Oz!" Gordy shouted.

I raced toward the horse, realizing half way there that I had no weapon of any kind. I did the only thing I could do. I grabbed the Dac's leg and pulled as hard as I could. I could see its mandibles nibbling on Gordy's neck. "Get off him, you rancid bug bite!"

My legs were swept out from under me by yet another Dac, a pig. It squealed and snorted. I swung wildly trying to fend it off, but it had a tight hold. I heard Lou scream. If anything could make her lose her human mask, this was it. If she was a Délon, I would know it soon enough.

The pig Dac bit me, and I yelped. I kept fighting with little success. I started to wonder where Devlin was when his future king needed him the most.

I managed to jab my elbow in the Dac's eye, distracting it for a brief moment. I had time to look around to see what was going on with the others. Gordy had managed to kick the dog Dac off the horse. It struggled to climb back on the horse's back and continue to feed on Gordy. Lou's horse was keeping a small Dac at bay. It looked like it could have been a cat in its previous life. Devlin was worse off than any of us. Five Dacs of various types were attacking him. He was holding his own, but barely, and he couldn't continue much longer.

A dog barked. A big dog. I turned toward the sound expecting to see another mutant Dac approach, but I couldn't have been more wrong or happier. It was Kimball. Not just Kimball. Wes's eight Taker killers were with my warrior dog. They ran down the highway like a stampeding army. The Dacs didn't have a chance.

Kimball leapt on the Dac that had set its sights on me. The two of them tumbled to the ground in a growling, snorting heap.

Two of the other dogs sunk their teeth into the Dac on Gordy's horse and yanked it to the pavement. They violently shook their heads, almost as if they were playing with a pet store toy. The Dac's leg ripped off.

Another of Wes's dogs grabbed the cat Dac that was attacking Lou and did what dogs do to cats they catch. The little Dac howled.

None of the dogs came to Devlin's rescue. The five remaining dogs barked and circled the Dacs and Devlin. It was clear the dogs were confused. They obviously had been trained to hate Délons, and they weren't very fond of Dacs either. They had no idea who to save or who to attack.

Kimball had disposed of the pig Dac. He ran to my side, panting, tail wagging, a goofy dog grin on his face. I knelt and hugged him around the neck. "Good boy." He barked. I stood. "Go help Devlin!" I pointed to the mass of Dacs and Devlin tearing the life out of each other. Kimball stepped toward them, but stopped. He turned and barked. It was clear he didn't want

Délon City

to help the Délon.

I heard the putter of a German-made vehicle approach. Wes's VW van came to a screeching halt behind us. He threw open the driver side door, and squeezed his portly frame out of the van. Valerie and Tyrone popped out of the back. They were armed with baseball bats. Wes had his trusty knife and something else. Something I was glad to see at the time, but later, when the little time travel episodes would play themselves over and over again in my head, I would regret having. He had J.J., my sword.

Wes whistled. "Kid." He tossed me the sword. Without hesitation I ran to help Devlin. The dogs followed. I swung J.J. and struck a Dac on the back. It diverted its attention from Devlin and turned on me. This Dac face was different. It was a deer – maybe. A dog took it down before it could lay a hand or hoof on me.

Wes barreled through the four Dacs still thrashing Devlin. His bulk caused two of them to collapse to the road. He swung his knife wildly and killed one of the Dacs. The other one squirmed out from under Wes and was immediately attacked by one of the dogs.

Devlin, left one-on-one with a Dac, wrapped his arms around the animal freak's neck and snapped it like a twig.

Within seconds the Dac attack was officially squelched. We were all alive. Some of us were bruised and bloodied, but we were still breathing.

"Yeah!" Gordy shouted. "Take that you filthy Dacs!" He slid off his horse. "We're bad, ahuh – we're b-a-d!"

Devlin stood motionless. "Shut up, human!" He started to sway. "You did nothing."

"It only looked like I was doing nothing. Those Dac butt munches fell right into my trap, my Délon friend, and oh by the way, I noticed you were getting your purple behind kicked from here to Timbuck..."

"Shut up!" Devlin didn't shout as much as he screamed uncontrollably. "I've lost my..." He looked at Wes. "Where did you come from?"

Wes didn't know how to answer. He turned to me. I shrugged my shoulders. "We were just driving by..." Wes started to say, but stopped when Devlin dropped to one knee.

"I cannot hear them." He fell face first onto the pitted concrete highway.

I stood stunned. "Devlin?"

He didn't answer.

"Ding dong the witch is dead!" Gordy said. He hooted and did a little dance. Devlin's right arm twitched. Gordy screeched and jumped back.

Lou walked over to Devlin and knelt down beside him. She examined him closely. "He's alive."

"Somebody stab him or hit him or shove fatty foods down his throat until he dies of a heart attack," Gordy said backing away. "Kill the purple piece of pus."

"Shut up, Gordy," I said. I motioned to Wes. "We need to get him in the van."

"You sure you want to do this, kid?" Wes said rubbing his stubbly chin.

"It's Devlin, Wes," I said.

"That ain't Devlin." He stuck the knife in the sheath clipped to his belt. "Not for a long while now."

"He will be again." Together we walked over to Devlin and dragged him to the van.

***

We found an unmanned convenience store at the next exit.

Délon City

It had been unmanned for a while. In fact, the closer we got to Délon City, the more homes, businesses, and churches we found that had been abandoned. It was as if everything close to the city was dead.

I sat in the manager's office with a bottle of hydrogen peroxide and wiped my wounds. I caught a glimpse of J.J. propped up against the wall, and was surprised that I was so happy to have it with me. It had belonged to Mr. Chalmers originally, but after everything we had been through together, that sword was mine.

My backpack lay next to it. As safe and secure as J.J. made me feel, the backpack, or rather what was inside the backpack, chilled me to the bone. I wanted to take my sword and stab it, but I'd never get away with it. It was connected to the Délon collective, and they would know the second I killed it.

I started thinking about our journey to this juncture. My mind flashed back to the mountains. Devlin had been behaving differently from that point on. He was less... less something. He had shrunk. I know it. What was it about the mountains? A snow flurry drifted through my mind's eye. It was cold on the mountains.

Suddenly, in my mind, I was back in Gordy's garage opening the freezer and looking at that dead shunter. The cold. Délons are cut off from each other in the cold. But it was cold in Tullahoma, and the Délons were fine.

It wasn't freezing, a voice said in my head. Thirty-two degrees.

I walked out of the manager's office and into the back storage area of the convenience store. I spotted what I was looking for immediately, a walk-in freezer. I raced to the front of the store praying all the way that Devlin was still unconscious.

Wes and Lou were reliving old times near the Lotto machine, Wes behind the counter stuffing a can of dip between his cheek and gums, and Lou perched on the counter eating a bag of

135

Cheetos.

"There he is," Wes said. "King of kings."

"Devlin," I said. "Where is he?"

"In the van," Wes replied. "Out like a tanked-up frat boy."

"We need to get him in here," I said. I went for the door.

"Now hold on... hold on." Wes gave Lou a look like I had lost my mind. "Them Délons is heavier that a ton of bricks with a ton bricks piled on top of them. Why in the world would we want to drag his purple butt up in here for?"

"I've got an idea," I said.

"Now I'm all kinds of happy for you there, Oz, but my old back's got some ideas of its own, and it ain't got nothing to do with lifting nothing heavy."

"What idea?" Lou asked.

I looked at her. She hadn't changed into a Délon during the Dac attack. She couldn't be one. I had no idea what Canter was mouthing off about in my trip to the future, but Lou wasn't a Délon. I suppose that didn't mean she wasn't a Délon spy, but she wasn't part of the collective at any rate.

"Délons don't like the cold," I said.

"Well, hell, anybody with a pea size brain knows that." Wes said.

"No, it's more than that. They lose themselves in the cold. They lose each other. They're not part of the collective. They may even become more human." I was so excited, I was talking a mile a minute.

"You've been out of the picture for a while now, junior," Wes said walking around the counter. "It don't get cold no more. Not winter cold. In fact, last year, right after you took out the Taker Queen, the temperatures did nothing but go up. Shirtsleeve weather from there on out. It'll dip in the forties from time to time, but thems some rare days."

Délon City

"It was cold on Monteagle yesterday," I said "Snowing, and the snow was sticking."

Lou thought it through. "You're right. I don't know why I didn't pay more attention to it, but it was."

"And Devlin's been different ever since," I said. "He's lost touch with the collective."

Wes grabbed a stick of beef jerky from a nearby canister. "Come to think of it, it has been a might colder this winter." He stuck the jerky in his mouth and tore off a chunk, all the while maintaining his dip of tobacco perfectly in his lower lip. "That don't explain why you want to drag that purple pile of crap in here."

"There's a walk-in freezer in the back."

"So," Wes said.

"So," Lou said jumping off the corner. "We need to get Devlin in the freezer."

"What good would that do?" Wes protested.

"It will tell us what freezing temperatures do to the Délons," I said. "It could be a way to beat them."

Wes gave it some thought. "What if it kills him? You willing to take that risk? You were keen on keeping him around before because he was Devlin."

I said, "It's a chance we have to take." I walked out of the convenience store before I could think about it. I was willing to sacrifice one of my old warriors for the greater good. I didn't want to give myself time to back out.

***

We put Devlin in the freezer and waited. Some of us waited better than others. The dogs lounged around in the convenience store parking lot. Kimball kept a close eye on his troops. Wes found a cot in the manager's office and decided he needed a nap. Gordy was busy bossing Valerie and Tyrone around. He had made the decision that he was not going to be last in the pecking order. As long as he barked orders at the two younger kids, he felt like he was in charge of something even though they weren't really listening to him.

Lou kept her distance from me. She had sensed that there was something wrong in our relationship. She didn't know what it was, but she knew I needed my space. I knew she wasn't a traitor. She couldn't be. I knew it in my heart of hearts, but I still needed some time alone to sort out what my next move would be.

I sat in the back storage area flipping through a Stephen King book that must have belonged to one of the former convenience store workers. It was *The Stand*, and it was as thick as a brick. It was about a super flu that wiped nearly everybody out. I could relate. There were good guys and bad guys and a whole lot of scary stuff on just about every page. I decided that once everything got back to normal I was going to read the book.

I leaned back on a box of toilet paper and to my surprise dozed off. It was unexpected. I was so tired I didn't even know I was tired. When I slept, I left that convenience store. I don't know where I went. I didn't dream. I just slept. It was a deep disappearing sleep, like I was invisible. I knew it was rare even while it was happening. I heard a voice in my head saying, "This is peace. Remember it."

The peace didn't last. I was torn from my deep sleep by the sound of Devlin screaming. I instinctively knew it was him. I stumbled to my feet and raced to the walk-in freezer. I was met there by the others.

"The poor sucker's awake," Wes said.

"You think?" Gordy said sarcastically.

Délon City

"What do we do?" Lou asked.

Tyrone and Valerie huddled together. They were both in mid-chew on candy bars scared out of their minds.

I cleared my throat. "I go in," I said.

"Wait a minute," Wes said. "Wait just a damn minute. That ain't the smartest idea you've ever had. You don't know what state he's in. If he's still a Délon, well then he's one pissed off Délon because we locked him in a freezer."

"Yeah," I said, "And if he's Devlin... Just plain Devlin, I mean, he's going to need our help, and we can't help him from this side of the door."

"Wes is right," Lou said. "You can't just walk in there." She reached into her jacket pocket and pulled out a small handgun. "Take this."

"Whoa!" Gordy said.

Tyrone stepped in closer. "Cool!"

Wes ripped the gun from her hand. "Cool, nothing. Where in tarnation did you get this thing?"

Lou cast her eyes down to the floor. A look of shame engulfed her. "I found it in the manager's office."

"A gun ain't nothing to be trifled with," Wes said. His voice was low and even, but his sense of outrage was evident. "If you ain't never used one of these things, you're more likely to kill yourself than what you're aiming at."

"A gun beats a knife any day," Gordy said smugly.

"Boy," Wes said stepping toward him. "I've had just about enough of your lip. I'm the adult here. You understand? What I say goes, and I say ain't none of you kids going to carry a gun." He turned to the freezer. "Step back. I'm going in."

"No," I protested.

"Son, that smart-ass friend of yours is right. A gun beats a knife any day of the week, and since I'm the only one here who's

139

fired one of these things before, I'm the one who's taking it into that freezer and seeing if old Devlin is a crazy-mad Délon or some poor little kid freezing his ass off."

"But," I said.

"But nothing. This ain't up for debate. You done a lot of leading up to this point, Oz, but it's my turn, you understand?"

I hesitated. I did understand. I knew he had to do this, and I knew why. I said nothing and backed away from the door.

Wes took a deep breath, gave his unshaven chin a stroke with his callused hand, and then opened the freezer door. "Close it behind me so... Nothing can get out." With that, he entered the freezer and Gordy quickly pushed the freezer door shut.

We waited for what seemed minutes, but was probably more like thirty seconds. There wasn't a sound from the other side of the door. At one point Lou put her hand on the door handle. I removed it gently. She tried to nod and smile, but she couldn't quite pull it off.

Gordy broke the silence. "Now that I think about it, I ain't too sure a gun will do much good against a Délon."

"Gordy," I said. "Shut up!"

"What?" he asked. "I'm just saying they got thick skin. Purple Pete's liable to get even madder if Mr. Redneck Goodwrench in there tries to shoot him."

"We should go in," Lou said.

"No! We wait!" I yelled it without conviction. I wanted to go in the freezer as much as she did.

The door opened. Wes's fat head popped out. "You best get in here," he said looking at me.

I swallowed and did as Wes requested. I stood in the doorway and peered through the fog of the chilled air. My eyes adjusted and I could see that the walls and shelves in the freezer were covered in oozing purple chunks of... Délon. "What..."

Délon City

"He exploded," Wes said. "Best I can figure anyway."

I dropped my head. "We killed him."

"We killed a Délon," Wes said. For the first time, I noticed Wes wasn't wearing his coat. He pointed to the back corner of the freezer. "But old Devlin is still alive and kicking."

Huddled in the corner, underneath Wes's coat, a naked Devlin trembled and cried silently. I rushed to him and knelt down. "Devlin!"

He looked up at me. He was covered in the purple ooze and it was starting to freeze. "Hey, boss man," he said.

"Devlin," I repeated. I didn't know what else to say. He was Devlin again. His chubby face was scarred a little and his eyes were still a little milky white, but I could make out the gray-blue tint around the pupils "You're back."

"I am?" he said. "Back?"

"You're not a Délon anymore." I looked up at Wes. "We need to get him out of here."

Devlin grabbed my arm. "Can't leave, boss."

"What do you mean you can't leave?"

"You're going to freeze to death in here, boy," Wes said.

"They'll find me out there," Devlin said. His trembling intensified.

"Who..." I corrected myself because I knew who. "How?"

"I can hear them out there," he said confused. "They've been looking for me... for us for a long time. We got cut off."

"Wes is right, you'll freeze to death in here."

"I'd rather freeze to death than have them find me," he answered. He twitched suddenly and tried to make himself smaller. "Don't let them find me."

I didn't know what to do. Leaving him in the freezer was cruel, but letting the Délon collective hone in on him outside the freezer seemed even crueler. I looked at Wes for guidance, but the

141

R.W. Ridley

expression on his face told me he was just as lost as I was.

I stood. "Let's find a towel or something to wipe that stuff off you, and then get you in some warm clothes at least."

He nodded.

Wes darted out of the freezer in search of a towel and clothes.

"They're losing control," Devlin said.

"What?" I asked.

"I'm the enemy, Oz. You need to interrogate me."

"You're Devlin. You're not the enemy."

"I'm a Délon... At least there's still a little Délon deep inside of me. You need to get all the information out of me before..." He stopped.

"Before what?"

"You know what."

"If you're talking about dying, I'm not going to let that happen..."

"Shut up, Oz!" His voice trembled from anger not the cold. "You can't save everybody. Your hero rap was getting tired when we were fighting the Takers. It's twice as bad and useless now. Worry about the people worth saving."

"You're not worth saving?"

"I'm a bad kid who did a few good things in his life. You should be fighting for the good kids who may have done a few bad things in their life."

"What's the difference?"

He laughed. "I have no idea. That's why I was never cut out for this hero crap."

Wes walked in with a towel and clothes. He tossed the towel to Devlin. "Wipe that mess off."

Devlin stood on wobbly legs and started to wipe himself down with the towel. "Like I said, they're losing control."

I cleared my throat. I didn't want to interrogate him, but he

Délon City

was right. "Why?"

"They don't know. They've ruled for almost a year now with no problems, but about a month ago the temperatures started to drop. They were able to keep them in the 90s until then."

"That's why they want their Source," I said.

"Exactly. They control the source, they control everything."

"What's the Source?" Wes asked.

"Don't know," Devlin said tossing the sloppy purple towel to the freezer floor. He stepped into a pair of long underwear. "None of them know either."

I looked at him finding myself not being able to believe that his stocky frame was a sleek Délon frame less than an hour ago. "But they think I know?"

"They think you're the key to everything."

"Me?"

"You're the way to the Source. That's all they know." He pulled on a pair of pants. His legs were visibly shaking, and he had to prop himself up against the wall.

"That's why they want to make me king?"

He chuckled. "They have no plans to make you king. Roy set his sites on that position from the beginning. He killed the Pure in order to become king, but the Royal Council turned him down flat until he finds the Source. Once he does, he's set."

"The Pure?" Wes asked.

"The Pure. The only pure Délon. He didn't start as a human. He was always Délon. You think Délons like me... or like I used to be are big uglies, you should have seen this guy. Makes Roy look like a boy scout. That's why the Royal Council looked the other way when Roy killed him, but they had no idea that the Pure held everything together."

"So, Roy kills the Pure, and the Délons lose control of their weather?" I asked.

"Not just the weather. Everything's out of control." Devlin wrapped himself in a big coat and sat on a five-gallon bucket labeled Friar Lard. "Dacs didn't show up until about a month ago. Skinners are multiplying faster than we can keep up. And you may have noticed the time shifts."

I nodded. "I noticed."

"None of that happened when the Pure was alive. He kept everything in line, if you know what I'm saying."

"I get the idea," I said. "So what do we do?"

"Oh no," he smiled. "I'm just the messenger. You're the hero. You've got to figure all that out on your own. The only thing I'll say is don't trust the time shifts. You don't always know when they're happening, and the people or freaks you meet in time shifts aren't always there to help you."

I sighed. I was running out of questions to ask him, and I knew once I did, I would have to decide what I was going to do with him. I wanted to put that off as long as possible. "What about..." I hesitated. I turned to Wes. "Can I have a minute alone with Devlin?"

Wes's face soured. He was hurt. "Sure." He backed out of the freezer.

I turned to Devlin. "What about the people?"

"The people?" he asked.

"Yeah, can I trust the people?"

"You got anyone specific in mind?"

I searched his cloudy eyes. "Lou. I mean what you just told me, it seems she should have known that. She's been with Roy and Reya all this time."

Devlin shook his head. "She's their personal cow. They only deal with her when they..."

"When they what?"

This time Devlin searched my eyes. "When they want to

feed?"

My stomach turned.

"Délons crave certain tastes, and certain tastes are reserved for the elite."

"Tastes?"

"Fear, hate, love," He grabbed my arm and pointed to my veins. "It's all running through your veins, and Délons crave it. They live to suck it out of you and taste it, even if it doesn't last."

"What was so special about Lou that Roy and Reya kept her around?"

"She has the one taste Délons crave most."

"What?"

"Hope."

***

"I'm not leaving him!"

"Damn it, Oz, you've got to stop hollering at me," Wes said. He was testing the air pressure on the tires of his VW bus. He was right. I don't know why I was yelling at him. He wasn't the idiot who refused to come out of the walk-in freezer. "That boy in there has been through about the worst kind of hell you can imagine. A body can't blame him for just wantin' to crawl up in the freezer and never come out."

"But I can protect him," I said.

He tapped the tire gauge with his index finger and peered up at me from his squatting position. "You're all kinds of smart and brave, Oz, but the truth is it'd take an army the size of Desert Storm to protect that kid. The Délons can't stand humans. I can only guess that they can't stand humans who used to be Délon even worse. They know all their secrets."

I paced in front of him. "There's got to be something we

can do." I racked my brain for a plan. There was an answer to this problem. I knew it. A thought came to me. "Tarak – he can help us."

"Not likely," Wes said standing. "He's got tunnel vision when it comes to stepping outside of his duties of protecting Nate. One hundred percent of his energies are focused in on that little fella'. That's why he ain't here now."

"Call him."

"Call him? He ain't got a phone you know."

"How do we get him here?"

Wes shrugged his shoulders. "He just shows up when he's supposed to."

"I want him to show up now," I was on the verge of throwing a tantrum like a little kid.

"Look here," Wes said in as stern a voice as I've ever heard him use. "It's about time you learned that wantin' something don't make it so. They's going to be times when you got to make tough choices, and as much as I hate to say it, this is one of them times."

My eyes started to well up from frustration. I didn't know what to do. I heard a high-pitched scream and laugh come from the other end of the parking lot. I turned to see Tyrone and Valerie kicking a ball they'd found in the convenience store. I had an idea. "The kids," I said.

"Son, there ain't nothing but kids here, you're going to have to be more specific"

"Valerie and Tyrone – they can stay and watch over Devlin." In my mind, it was the perfect solution.

"No," Wes said flatly. "Not a snowball's chance in hell."

"Yes," I replied, my voice rising above his. "He needs somebody to stay behind. He's going to run out of food."

"And what if trouble comes? Tyrone and Valerie will be left

to fend for themselves. I ain't going to have that." His face was turning red.

"They can take care of themselves," I said. "They're warriors."

"They was kids two seconds ago," he responded. The veins in his neck were bulging. He was getting angrier by the second.

"You know what I mean," I said.

"No I don't because you don't know what you mean!" His voice had finally risen to the level of a yell.

Lou and Gordy stepped out of the convenience store to investigate. The dogs, Valerie and Tyrone – all eyes had shifted to us.

"Then you tell me what to do," I snapped back.

"Leave him," Wes barked. His voice rang through my ears.

I stood as I felt the earth spinning out of control. I couldn't even tell if I had a heartbeat anymore. My breathing was labored. I think this is what my mother used to call a panic attack. I would have fallen to the ground if Wes hadn't caught me. I heard the footsteps of the others running toward us. I shook my head and gathered my thoughts. I wanted to be standing on my own before the others reached us. Wes let go. He understood that I had to stand on my own. I breathed in through my nose and exhaled deeply through my mouth. It was over as quickly as it came.

"Oz, dude, you all right?" Gordy asked as he approached.

"You should sit down," Lou suggested.

"I'm fine," I said. "We need to hit the road. They're expecting us." I turned to Wes. "You'll follow. Not too close. Have you figured out how to get in the city?"

He looked at me confused. He wasn't sure if the Devlin issue was resolved. "Tarak gave us a contact. Another Keeper. He... or it will know how to contact you once we're inside the city."

"Then that's that," I said. I walked toward the horses.

"What about Devlin?" Lou asked.

R.W. Ridley

Without stopping I said, "We're leaving him."

THIRTEEN

Y ou smell Délon City before you see it. Actually, you can almost see the smell it's so pungent. The odor was a mixture of raw sewage, burning rubber, and decay. When I got my first glance at the twisted hulk of a city, it looked like it smelled... rotten.

The city was under a dome of death. Carcasses, animal, human, insect, and Délon were woven together into an enormous, macabre shield that surrounded the entire city.

Upon first seeing it, I stopped Chubby. The shunter in my backpack must have sensed we were near the city because it vibrated, twitched, and screeched like never before. I had thought about sticking the little blob in the walk-in freezer with Devlin, but General Roy would have known I didn't have it with me the second I set foot in Délon City. I would have to deal with the little face sucker when it finally emerged. There was just no way around it.

Gordy rode on, mouth agape, unable to fathom what he was seeing. Lou continued on nonplussed. This was old hat to her. It was so unremarkable to her that she didn't even think to mention it to us, to warn us of the horror of it all.

It took her several seconds to realize that I was no longer riding beside her. She looked over her shoulder and saw my appalled expression. She quickly turned her horse and galloped toward me.

"I tell myself it's not real," she said.

I was dazed. "What?"

"I tell myself that Oz Griffin will make this all go away. He got rid of the Takers. He can get rid of the Délons."

I shifted my gaze from the death dome to her brown eyes.

"That's how I've been able to survive all this. That's how I can look at that horrible thing day after day. I knew you'd come back, Oz. I knew it." She motioned to Délon City. "That place doesn't exist. One of these days, soon, I'm going to be back on my family's RV headed towards Disney World just like I was before this all started, and you're going to make that happen, Oz."

I swallowed hard. "What makes you so sure?"

"Because," she said. "Because I know." She turned her horse back around and headed for the entrance of the city.

Gordy turned to me and shook his head. His eyes pleading. He waited for me to abort the mission and just ride back to Tullahoma as fast as I could. I disappointed him and pressed forward.

The entrance to Délon City was big enough for a tractor trailer to enter. Both sides of the dome opening were guarded by no less than twenty Délons. They watched us enter, but never approached. I was surprised at the variety of their appearance. They were all tall and lean, and they all had the typical spider leg hairdo, but some of them had spider leg beards. I looked for signs that this gave them rank over the others, but it didn't seem to make a difference.

Lou led us through the now darkened highway. The dome ceiling blacked out the sun, but the temperature inside the city was at least 20 degrees warmer than outside.

The massive skyscrapers that made up Atlanta's horizon were still present, but they were dying shells of what they once were. A dark purple soot seemed to cover every inch of their exterior.

Abandoned cars, buses, and trucks riddled the highways, just as they had when the Takers were in control, only now half of

Délon City

them were set on fire. I guessed they were used to help keep the temperatures up in the city.

Between the smoke and the smell, it was not easy to breathe, but we managed somehow. Gordy coughed and hacked more than Lou or me, but much to his credit, he kept on pace with us without a word of complaint. It may have been that he was afraid of being left behind if he stopped to protest. After all, we'd left Devlin behind.

There were Délons by the thousands - the tens of thousands even. They were literally crawling all over each other like a colony of army ants. Every once in a while a pair of dead eyes would focus on us as we rode through the streets of Délon City. A Délon would raise its head in our direction and sniff and then return to doing whatever it was doing.

I even saw the occasional Taker. They were obviously subservient to the Délons. If I had to guess, they were being used as slave labor. The spoils of victory. Only the Délons were victorious because I killed the Taker Queen. Never did I regret that more than riding through the streets of Délon City. I had made a terrible mistake. If I had it to do over again, I wouldn't do it again.

About an hour after we entered the city, we finally arrived at our destination, 30 Peachtree Plaza. It was a nondescript 20-story building, but the walls of the building were alive with scores of Délons crawling all over each other to the top of the building and back down. It looked like a pointless exercise on their part, but it must have served a purpose.

"We're here," Lou said.

"Where?" Gordy asked in between a hack and a cough.

"General Roy's headquarters."

"Great," Gordy coughed. "We've seen it. Can we go home now?"

"Our guests!" A voice boomed. Roy stood at the top of the stairs leading to the front door. "We've been waiting!" He descended the stairs. I could see his eyes moving as he scanned our numbers. "You're one short... A Délon short."

I could hear Gordy swallow. He scooted back in his saddle. Lou looked to me to reply. It was then I wished I had prepared a lie for this inevitable situation. Not a lie exactly. The Délons would detect that. When the truth will get you in a heap of trouble, just give them the facts. That's what my grandfather used to say.

"We were attacked by Dacs," I said. "We lost Devlin." Those were the facts.

"Where?"

"Outside of Dalton."

The general reached the bottom of the stairs and stopped. He raised his hand. The crawling Délons stopped. They focused on Roy. He flicked his wrist to the right, and a hundred or so Délons broke off from the once crawling mass. They approached their general in uniform columns of four. He flicked his wrist to the left, and the columns sprinted toward the city's entrance.

General Roy smiled. "He will be avenged."

"We took care of that," I said. "I mean we already killed the Dacs."

He cocked his head and studied us. "Really, just the three of you?"

I didn't answer.

"You are a great warrior." He laughed. "There are more to kill," he said. "On that you can rely." He held out his hand and motioned us to dismount. "Come, come, I have a few surprises for you."

The three of us dismounted and slowly made our way to the front door of the building. General Roy held the door for us. When we entered, a sour looking Reya was waiting for us on the other side. She found it impossible to hide her disdain for me.

"Welcome," she said with no feeling at all.

I didn't bother returning the fake nicety. Délon Miles waited for us on the elevator. He never questioned where Devlin was. They were inseparable as humans. Now, Miles couldn't care less where his old friend was.

The six of us rode to the top floor. The elevator doors opened and we stepped into a hallway lined on both sides by Délons. They stood at attention while we walked by with the general, but it felt like a lot of them were looking at Lou, Gordy, and me as food.

Knowing now that the general had concocted the whole king scenario to trick me into leading them to their Source made me feel vulnerable. As soon as he determined I was useless, we were all dead. I hoped to be out of the city long before then. I was here to get Ajax. How I was going to do that, I didn't know.

We reached the end of the hallway and stood in front of a set of double doors. "Your accommodations," General Roy said. With a nod of his grotesque head, he ordered Miles to open the doors.

It was an enormous penthouse condominium that was probably one of the premier properties when Délon City was Atlanta. Basically it was intact. The stench of the city still seeped through the walls, but if you just saw it in a photograph you would be wowed. It had marble floors throughout, four bedrooms, five bathrooms, a view of the city that was currently obstructed by Délons crawling up and down the building. The furniture, although covered in the telltale transparent purple slime, looked expensive, like the stuff my mom used to pine over in catalogs.

"I trust this will do," General Roy said.

"Boy, oh boy," Gordy replied. "It is good to be king, huh, Oz?"

"Yeah," I said flatly.

"Well, we'll let you rest up from your trip," Roy said guiding Reya and Miles back in the hallway. "We have a special dinner for you tonight with some special guests."

"Who?" I asked.

"No, no," Roy said. "It's a surprise."

"What about the football game?" Gordy asked.

"Cancelled," Roy smiled. "In Oz's honor. We have something much more entertaining in store."

The three Délons stood outside the doorway looking in the apartment as if we were some exhibit in a zoo. "Come, Lou," General Roy said. Miles and Reya practically licked their chops.

Lou's chin dropped and she stepped toward them. I held out my arm and stopped her. "She stays."

"We have plans for her," Roy said, the irritation in his voice was apparent.

"I have plans for her," I said.

"She is ours, human," Reya snapped. General Roy gave her a stern glare.

"Not tonight," I said. I wasn't about to let them have their favorite snack.

I could see the spider legs on General Roy's head twitch, but he fought to keep himself under control. "Very well." They exited the condo, but not without Reya giving me one last look of total contempt.

"Whoa, bro," Gordy said. "That Délon chick does not like you, man."

"She never has..." We were interrupted by a loud popping sound. I felt a thump against the middle of my back. "What the...?" A wet, oozing warmth began to spread up and down my spine. "You guys feel that?"

"Feel what?" Gordy asked.

"Take off your backpack," Lou demanded.

Délon City

"What?" I couldn't imagine why she was so insistent.

"Take it off!" She didn't wait for me to comply. She grabbed one of the shoulder straps and yanked it down.

The shunter.

I wriggled and turned and jumped as if I were on fire. "Get it off! Get it off! Get it off!" I could feel its jellyfish tentacles probing through the thick material of the backpack.

I finally slipped both arms through the shoulder straps and let the now soaked backpack fall to the floor. Gordy jumped up on a nearby chair while Lou ran to the kitchen. She returned with a cleaver. I cursed myself for leaving J.J. on Chubby's saddle.

"What do we do? What do we do?" Gordy shouted.

"Why are you so scared?" I asked. "I'm the marked one."

"Yeah, but you heard Devlin," he said. "If it can't find the marked, it'll latch onto pretty much anything and suck its brains out."

"Can't find the marked? I'm right here!"

"Oh," Gordy said. "Yeah, right." I could feel the terror drain from his body once he realized he was no longer in danger.

A tiny hole appeared on the backpack and a thread thin tentacle stretched out of it.

Lou stood at the ready with the cleaver. Every fiber of her being wanted to raise it above her head and bring it crashing down on the squirmy little shunter, but she knew as soon as she did the Délons outside the window would come storming in.

"The kitchen," I said. "We can put it in the freezer." I picked the backpack up by one of its straps and held it at arm's length. A second tentacle had burrowed another hole in the thick fabric. I hurried across the marble floor through the formal dining room and pushed opened the swinging door to the kitchen. The refrigerator was in sight when the third and fourth tentacles ripped through the backpack. The shunter was tearing it to shreds.

155

Lou zipped around me, and ran to the refrigerator. Gordy chose not join to us. I pictured him casually reading a Sports Illustrated on the couch, not giving us a second thought. We would have to have a serious talk about teamwork.

Lou opened the freezer and began tossing out all the frozen food items left by the previous owners. The shunter had torn a flap in the backpack. I could see its jelly like body. If it had eyes, it would have been peering out at me. I could hear the fabric of the backpack ripping.

"Hurry," I said

"There's a lot of crap in here," Lou answered. "Some of it's frozen to the sides of the freezer."

I put the backpack down on a nearby counter. "Here," I said. "Let me."

Somewhat insulted, Lou stood and let me try to remove the items stuck to the sides of the freezer. I knelt down and tugged at a carton of ice cream. I could feel Lou's sense of satisfaction when I couldn't budge it. I gave it a more forceful yank and the entire shelf came out while I stumbled backwards to the kitchen floor. A cascade of frozen food came tumbling out of the freezer. It wasn't pretty, but it got the job done.

There was no time to pat myself on the back. I jumped up and raced to the counter where I had left the backpack. I knew I was running out of time. I picked it up, and almost had a heart attack when the solifipod rolled out of a huge gaping hole in the backpack. The shunter had torn through the pack, and what's worse, neither Lou nor I knew where it was.

"Oh boy," I said.

Lou held her cleaver at the ready. "This is not good."

I searched the surrounding area for a weapon. "Next time," I said, "don't let me leave J.J. with the horses." I opened a drawer and found a rolling pin. It would have to do.

Délon City

We heard the sound of thousands of little tentacles scampering across the floor.

"Do you see it?" I asked.

"No, but I hear it," Lou answered.

We were back to back now, slowly circling and looking in every direction.

"I'm really getting tired of creepy crawlies," I said.

The shunter let out a series of chirps. My left eye twitched in response. I frantically started kicking the frozen food items away from the freezer. The little face sucker was about to make its move, and I didn't want anything obstructing the door. Whatever was going to happen was going to happen fast.

"Got any ideas?" Lou asked.

"Not really," I said. "Nothing to do but wait..." I stopped mid-sentence. The room started to spin as the chirping got louder. The twitching in my eye spread throughout my whole body. I fell to my knees and dropped the rolling pin.

"Oz?" Lou said. Her voice was shallow and distant. I heard her scream. No, it wasn't her screaming. It was the shunter. A flash of bright white hit me. Lou stood over me. Another flash of bright white.

"What the hell?" It was Gordy's voice.

Everything went black.

***

When I came to, I was lying on a couch. It took me a minute to get my bearings. I was in the penthouse condo. I had just been in the kitchen. How did I get here? I turned to the right. Lou was sitting on the coffee table staring at me. She had a red welt that stretched diagonally across her face.

"What happened?" I asked.

"It's called the shunter's song," Lou said. "It subdues the marked with a series of chirps."

"You went down like a sack of potatoes," Gordy said. He leaned over the back of the couch and stared down at me. "Lucky for you I'm here."

"Please," Lou said disgusted. "I had to beg you to help."

"Whatever," Gordy barked. "Who helped you get that thing in the freezer?"

"You shut the door. I put it in the freezer."

"Is that where you got that welt?" I asked trying to sit up.

Lou put her hand on my shoulder and gently pushed me back down. "Stay down."

"The point is," Gordy said. "I didn't want to get any marks on me, because then I'd have some explaining to do to the general at dinner. How're you going to explain your face and your hand, little miss smarty pants?"

"Hand?" I scanned for Lou's hand, but she kept it hidden under a towel. "Let me see."

"It's not that bad," she said.

"Let me see," I insisted.

She hesitated and pulled the towel back. Her hand was swollen to twice its size and it was fire red. "It doesn't hurt that much." I could tell she was lying.

I sat up without any difficulty this time. "Gordy, go in the kitchen and get a pack of frozen peas or corn or something. There's a bunch of frozen food on the floor."

"The kitchen? Why me?" His voice was beginning to grate on me like fingernails on a chalkboard. "That thing's in there."

"It's dead in the freezer," I said. "Go now!"

He could tell by my tone the next request would come with a fist to the face. "All right, but I'm getting tired of people bossing me around." He stomped off toward the kitchen.

Délon City

I carefully took Lou's swollen hand in mine. "What happened?"

"Shunter's have stingers you want to try to avoid." She smiled. "I tried." She cringed as I examined the hand.

"What happened? I mean after I blacked out?"

"The shunter leapt off the counter and lashed its tail like a whip. That's where I got this." She pointed to the welt on her face. "I caught it before it hit you, and stuffed it in the freezer. Gordy helped a little." She smiled.

I smiled back. "I know him better than that." Something in my stomach quivered as I discovered I liked holding Lou's hand in mine. It made me feel uneasy and happy at the same time.

Gordy burst back into the living room holding a melting bag of peas. "It ain't exactly frozen." He tossed it on the coffee table. I picked it up and placed it on Lou's swollen hand.

"Keep this on it for the next twenty minutes or so," I said. She nodded, biting her lip. The pain was getting worse. I stood up. "Your turn to lie down." I helped her to the couch.

"What about me?" Gordy asked. "When do I get to rest?

"Shut up, Gordon," I said. I grabbed him by the collar and pulled him into the dining room. "You're working on my last nerve."

"Relax, Oz. Relax." His eyes were open wide, and sweat was forming on his forehead.

"What do you know about the shunter's sting?"

"Me? Nothing... I don't know nothing."

I tossed him backward and he fell onto a chair. "What do you know?"

"What makes you think I know anything?"

"Because you knew how to kill it. You seem to know an awful lot that you're not telling me. Now, I'm going to ask you one more time. What do you know about the shunter's sting?"

He sat up in the chair, and straightened his collar. "It hurts like a mother," he said.

"Tell me something I don't know." I rushed him.

He shouted. "Wait! Wait! Wait!"

I stopped.

He lowered his voice. "She'll be dead in three days — maybe four."

"What?" I had to fight the urge to punch him repeatedly. "That's not true. Tell me that's not true."

"You asked me what I know. That's what I know." His voice started to squeak.

My heart stopped. I plopped down on the chair next to him. My mouth went dry, and my eyes started to burn. "It's not true," I whispered. I felt ashamed for ever doubting her loyalty to me. I turned away from Gordy so he couldn't see the tears roll out of my eyes. "Is there a cure?"

Gordy snickered. "The Délons aren't big on curing things, Oz. They prefer it when things just die."

"Then we'll treat it like a snake bite," I said, a little bit of hope seeping into my voice.

"This ain't no snake bite," Gordy responded. "That poison hit her brain about two seconds after that thing stung her. I seen it before. Maggie Capp — you remember — from Camp Summer Tree — she got stung when them solifipods and shunters started showing up around Tullahoma. A little purple jellyfish face hatched from a slimy solifipod. Didn't none of us know what it was at the time. She tried to pet it. Can you believe that? The girl actually tried to pet the ugly mess." His gaze drifted off like he was actually standing next to Maggie Capp, reliving the entire episode. "Anyway that little bag of jelly whipped out its stinger and stung her quicker than a dart hits its target. Her pop thought the same thing you did, treat it like a snakebite. He took out his pocketknife, sliced a little 'x' over the bite and started sucking." Gordy stopped telling the story, but continued to stare off into space.

"Well?" I said.

"Hmmm?" He focused back on me. "Oh, she died three days later." He stood up. "Her old man died two days after that. The docs said both their brains just liquefied."

This time my heart shattered into a million little pieces. I swallowed the lump that was forming in my throat. I didn't want to believe what Gordy was telling me. Maybe he was the 'G' I wasn't supposed to trust after all. Maybe, just maybe, he was trying to demoralize me so I couldn't go on.

"That sucked," Gordy said. "I mean, Maggie dying and all. I kind of liked her. Did I ever tell you that she and I french kissed the last time we were at Camp Summer Tree?"

I managed a chuckle. "Only about a million times. I don't think there's a kid in our class you didn't tell."

He smiled. "Man, she was pretty." He put his hand on my shoulder. "If I'd been you, I probably would have found a way to save her."

Shocked by his confidence in me, I turned to see that tears were rolling down his cheek. I nodded and stood. Before heading to the dining room door I said, "Thanks."

"For what?" he asked.

"For being somebody I can trust." I exited the room.

FOURTEEN

I was not going to let Lou die, and I wasn't going to save her by hanging out in the penthouse condo, so I told Gordy to keep an eye on her, and I left in search of... what I don't know. I just knew there had to be answers somewhere on the streets of Délon City.

When I stepped out the front door of the building, the crawling Délons took notice of me. My movement was being recorded and passed on from Délon to Délon. General Roy probably already knew I was no longer resting up for dinner in the comfort of the penthouse. I wondered if he cared.

I should have been worried for my safety, but I wasn't. Somehow I knew no harm would come to me. After all, General Roy needed me. He wasn't going to let his underlings hurt me. I just hoped they were all on the same wavelength.

A Délon approached. "General Roy would like to know if you require an escort." The purple pile of puss was not familiar to me at all. I didn't know him when he was human. Spider leg tentacles covered his head and half his face.

"I'm fine."

He waved his hand to a group of Délons on the street corner. One broke away from the pack, and within minutes returned with Chubby.

"You're under the general's protection," the Délon said. "We'll

Délon City

be watching you."

I didn't know if that was a friendly gesture or a threat. I mounted Chubby, and tried to accept the fact that General Roy would know my every move. He couldn't know that Lou was stung by my now dead shunter. He would feed her to the skinners for stuffing it in the freezer. I had to do the impossible. I had to operate in secret in plain view of my enemy.

Chubby plodded down the street seemingly as nervous as I was. The flow of Délons crawling all over each other went back and forth from us to the general's headquarters. They were literally reporting on our every move. Ahead of us, the dead eyes of thousands of Délons bore holes into our backs as we traveled from block to block.

As I turned the corner on Peachtree Avenue to Peachtree Lane, a mass of Délons broke off from the horde and turned up the street. A series of grunts and roars filled the blackened air. A familiar chill traveled through my body. I had to fight Chubby to keep moving forward.

Ahead of us, the group of Délons who broke away from the collective, squatted and prepared for an attack. The ground shook, and a sinkhole formed just in front of the Délons. Five Takers emerged from the hole, claws out, snarls across their massive jaws.

The Délons struck without hesitation. They outnumbered the Takers five to one, but each Taker was more than twice the size of a single Délon, so the Takers were able to hold their own. I watched with unexpected delight as Délon after Délon fell.

Chubby stopped about twenty feet away from the action. He nervously shifted his weight from left to right. He fought the urge to turn and run. My attention was divided between the battle in front of us and Chubby's obvious agitation.

"Whoa, boy, it's all right. Calm down."

He whinnied, raised up on his back legs, and came back down.

"Keep it together, Chubs!"

He whinnied and jerked up. This time I fell to the concrete road flat on my back. The fall forced the air out of my lungs. I couldn't catch my breath. I felt the ground rumble beneath me. A cracking noise faintly made its way into my consciousness. Chubby galloped back down the street, away from the chaos. Just as I was regaining my ability to breathe, the street beneath me gave way and I fell down a massive sinkhole. I heard the Délons squeal and sound out the alarm. A Taker's clawed hand swooped in and grabbed me by my face and dragged me down a homemade tunnel.

***

I don't know how long I was dragged. I struggled to free myself from the Taker's vise-like grip with no success. The tunnel closed in as we passed through so it was impossible for the Délons to follow.

This was it. I was one dead kid. Forget about seeing my fifteenth birthday. The Takers were going to have their revenge. I knew now that the attack of the five Takers was a distraction to get to me. They were going to tear me limb from limb. All I could think of while the slimy Greasywhopper was dragging me through the tunnel was that I'd failed Lou. She was going to die because I allowed myself to get killed.

We reached an opening to the tunnel. I found myself lying on concrete again. The smell of car fumes and gasoline lingered in the air. The Taker let go of me. I surveyed the area and discovered that being dragged by the face gives you a sore neck.

The Taker had brought me to an underground parking garage. I stood on uneasy legs. It towered over me. It snapped its massive jaws and lightly shoved me back. It began to chatter, a noise I had heard too many times in my life. It shoved me again.

"What do you want? Eat me, if you're going to eat me!"

It shoved me again.

"What?"

Frustrated, it gave me a harder shove. I realized then that it wanted me to turn around. I complied and almost jumped for joy when I saw Wes's van.

"They're here! They made it!" I ran to the van, but much to my disappointment, it was empty.

"Where are they?" I turned to interrogate the Taker, but it was gone.

"They're safe." The unknown voice bounced off the concrete walls of the parking garage.

"Who's there?"

"I am Newell." A Délon like I had never seen before stepped out of the darkness. Its skin was jet black and its eyes were purple. Its spider leg tentacles were hidden underneath a white cloak. "The second Keeper."

"A good guy, right?" I backed away as it approached me.

"There is no good or bad. There is only that which should be."

"Okay, then let me put it this way, you're not going to eat me, kill me, or turn me into something that looks like you, are you?"

He smiled, and I didn't get the creepy vibe I got from a typical Délon smile. "No. That's not my plan, but you could do worse than look like me. The ladies really dig this white robe."

"It's not the robe I'm worried about." I slowly felt at ease. "Where are my friends?"

"They are farther underground."

"I want to see them.

"There's no time. The Délons are already on their way." He removed his hood and revealed a thick main of white spider leg tentacles.

"Why did you bring me here?" I asked.

"To tell you to get out." He circled me as he spoke. "This isn't your fight. This time belongs to my warrior."

I scratched my head. "Gee, if I remember correctly your warrior was captured by our friends the Takers back there." I motioned toward a group of the slimy monsters standing in the shadows. "Then when I... when the Délons took over, they kept him under lock and key."

"It doesn't concern you." He raised his voice. "The rules must be observed. And the rules say you are not the warrior for this time, this world! Leave this city!"

"Doesn't concern me?" It was my turn to raise my voice. "Are you mental? This is my planet, Newell. You freaks are the ones who have to go. I can't help it if your boy warrior got himself caught. I did my part, and I'll step up to the plate again." I was being a little cockier than I normally would have been, but I was tired of the "rules" line.

He breathed deeply, calmed himself, and spoke in much softer tones. "If you interfere, you will disrupt the balance. My warrior must defeat the Délons."

"How's he going to do that from prison?" I asked.

"It is a matter of faith, young Oz." Newell's spider leg hair bristled, and his insect mandibles made their first appearance as he opened his mouth. They snapped wildly. He was clearly nervous.

"What?"

"The Délons are near," he said. "You must go from here, from this city. Go back to Tullahoma."

"What do you think I'll be going back to? My parents are gone. Everyone is... I have no choice but to fight this fight."

A total look of exasperation washed over his face. "You will fail, and Lou will die."

Délon City

My heart jumped at the mention of Lou's name. "Do you know how to save her?"

He started to slink back in the darkness. "I must have your word that you will not interfere with this battle. For this promise, I will tell you how to save Lou."

I thought it over. I shouldn't have hesitated. It should have been an easy choice for me to make, but it was hard for me to let go of the fight. I wanted the Délons gone, and I wasn't at all confident that Newell's warrior was up to the task.

I heard the clatter of Délons approaching. I had to make a decision. "Okay," I shouted. "Deal!"

"A second sting will save her," he said. "Either from the same shunter or from a shunter in the same line." With that he disappeared into the darkness, and a group of Takers stepped forward. They hunched down and growled like rabid dogs. When the Délons arrived, the Takers lunged for me, but the Délons were on them before they could touch me. It was a show. The Takers were completing the ruse that they had kidnapped me to kill me. They were sacrificing themselves to make it look legitimate. They were giving their lives for the greater good. I had not expected that from Takers. I had no idea they were capable of such nobility.

In contrast, I felt like I had sacrificed the world to save Lou. As I made my way back to street level with my Délon escorts, I tried to decide if that was noble or not. Lou herself had told me to do whatever it takes to defeat the Délons, and I caved at the first sign of trouble.

As a Délon met me at the curb holding onto Chubby's reigns, I decided it didn't matter. All that mattered was that I was going to save Lou's life. I didn't care if that was smart or not. There was no way I was ever going to let her die.

I kicked Chubby in the ribs and raced back to the general's headquarters to save my friend.

FIFTEEN

The general's huge dining table took up most of the lobby of the condominium. Reya and the Royal Council, five Délons dressed in overly decorated black robes, were seated when Gordy and I arrived. I had the shabbily repaired backpack that housed my now dead shunter draped over my shoulder. The center of the table was crawling with screamers, no serving platters, just thousands of the high-pitched worms wriggling in the middle of the table.

"Dude," Gordy whispered. "I'm telling you right now if that's dinner then I'm just going to start puking now to save some time."

A Taker entered the room carrying a plate of moldy bread and small containers of chocolate pudding.

"So much for filling up on the bread," I said. "At least there's pudding."

"Oh man, I hope that's pudding," Gordy said wide-eyed.

We took our seats, and I placed the backpack on the floor next to me. The Royal Council looked uneasy to be sitting at a dinner table with two human guests. My guess is that they were used to the humans being one of the courses.

"The girl," Reya said. "Where is she?"

"Tired," I said. "We had a rough trip."

A member of the Royal Council to my left groaned. "Insolence. She was invited to dine with the general. She should be here."

Délon City

My blood boiled. "She's not feeling well."

The Royal Councilman continued. "Not feeling well... appalling. She should be disciplined."

"Hey," I shouted. "Spidey-doo, leave it alone. She's not here. Deal with it!"

I didn't have to look at Gordy to know that he was shaking.

The Royal Councilman didn't respond. He sat still and seethed. He wanted my head on a stick, but he knew the general needed me. He finally faked a smile and said, "A discussion for another time, perhaps."

It was a small, false victory because as soon as they determined I didn't have the information they needed, they would kill me. But for the time being, it felt good watching the purple puke back down.

General Roy and Miles entered the lobby. Everyone except Gordy and me stood respectfully. The general took notice, but he let it pass without a word. He motioned for everyone to sit while he stood by his chair. He reached down and scooped up a handful of wriggling screamers. "We welcome our honored guests," he said and then stuffed the worms in his mouth. The other Délons followed suit.

Gordy and I watched uncomfortably as they chowed down. I heard Gordy belch and cover his mouth. I was sure he was fighting the urge to purge.

The front door to the building opened, and I turned to watch a crab-like creature enter the lobby. It was Canter. I knew it without being introduced.

"Ahh, our good friend, Canter," General Roy said. "Come, come, join us."

The creature moved silently and fluidly to our table. He wore the tongue around his neck. He did not say a word, but I could hear him in my head. "Young, Oz. We finally meet."

169

I nodded. We had met before, but I wasn't exactly sure if meeting in a time-shift counted. Maybe he didn't even remember. I stared at the tongue hanging from his neck.

"Gorilla," he said. "I tore it from a true freak of nature, a talking gorilla."

I stood. "Gorilla?"

A cackle sounded off in my head. "A friend of yours?"

I lunged toward him, but Gordy stepped in front of me. "Easy, Oz. Don't go all cowboy on me."

"Where is he?" I shouted. "Where's Ajax?"

The general mumbled with a mouth full of screamers, "Ajax? Ahhh, don't make me ruin the surprise."

"Surprise?"

He shook his head. "Yes, tomorrow... instead of the same old tired game of football we've scheduled a one-on-one match... There, I've said too much. I really don't want to say any more." He continued to stuff screamers in his mouth. "I've arranged for you and your party to sit with me in my luxury box tomorrow, along with Canter and your parents."

"My parents?"

"That is what they're called, isn't it?" The general asked. "I have such a hard time with the human terminology."

"They're here?"

"They are," he said snapping his fingers. Miles and another Délon escorted my mother out into the lobby. She could barely stand on her own. A purple rash covered half her face. I ran to her. "Mom!" Her eyes were dull and lifeless. She didn't recognize me. I turned to the general. "The transformation is killing her."

He smiled. "Yes. Some take to it better than others. There's really no explanation for it." He stuffed more screamers in his mouth.

I took my mother's arm and guided her to a nearby chair.

Délon City

"Don't worry, mom. Everything is going to be okay." She shifted her dead gaze to me, slowly lifted her arm, and managed to point a crooked index finger toward the dinner party. "Food," she said weakly.

I gulped. "Yeah, food." I turned to Miles and mustered up the strength to say, "Bring my mother some food." He complied.

"My father," I said still tending to my mother. "Where is he?"

"Don't call me that," said the other Délon who had entered with my mother and Miles.

I turned to the strange Délon. "Pop?"

He snarled.

"Manners, new one," General Roy said. "The boy is to be your king."

The Délon who used to be my father heeded the general's warning and cast me a menacing grin. "My king."

Meanwhile my mother took a handful of screamers from Miles and shoveled them in her mouth like she hadn't eaten in a week. I couldn't watch. I went back to my seat.

Gordy had torn the top off a container of pudding and was sniffing the contents. He dipped a finger in the brown gel and carefully licked it. He sighed. "It's pudding."

Canter approached him, beamed a thought into Gordy's head, and then silently moved around to the general's end of the table. Gordy eyed him with a look of horror. He sat motionless with a glob of chocolate pudding on the end of his finger.

"What's wrong with you?" I asked.

Gordy swallowed. "Dude, he just told me I have a beautiful tongue."

"Oh... well..." I didn't know what to say, so I decided to leave it at that, an unfinished thought about a disturbing compliment from a half-man, half-crab thingy. Man, my life was getting really weird.

The chatter around the table picked up. The Délons were talking amongst themselves. They paid less and less attention to Gordy and me as the night went on. They filled their bellies with screamers and drank what smelled like rotten milk. I managed to eat one small container of pudding, while Gordy ate five before he started complaining of a stomachache. Time was ticking, and Lou's chances of survival were getting slimmer by the minute.

I picked up my backpack and stood up. "Excuse me," I said, but no one heard me. They were too caught up in their Délon world. "Excuse me," I said again. Still no response. Frustrated, I opened the backpack and dumped the dead shunter on the table. "Excuse me," I shouted. The Délons gasped, and Canter looked on almost amused.

"What is this?" General Roy said spitting bile.

"A dead shunter. Mine actually," I said.

He began to tremble with rage. "What have you done?"

The other Délons started to hiss. Their spider legs were going crazy.

"Nothing," I said. "It just died."

General Roy bellowed a rumbling groan. He raised a fist and brought it down on the table, breaking off a piece of the thick wooden surface.

"I told you this wasn't a good idea," Gordy whispered.

"Shhhh," I said.

"This is indefensible!" a member of the Royal Council shouted.

"We should tear his eyes out," another one added.

"Whoa, fellas," I said. "Hold on. Your shunter here is defective. I just need a new one. That's all."

Délons from outside started to pour into the building, one angrier than the next. I knew they would want to kill me, but I had convinced myself when I was coming up with this plan that I could talk my way out of it. I was really beginning to doubt that now.

"Shunters just don't die," Reya practically screamed.

"This one did," I said. "Didn't it, Gordy."

Gordy was too scared to speak. He was backing away from the table.

"Think about it," I said. "Why would I bring the thing down here if I killed it? Not for a pat on the back, I can tell you that much. It died, get it. I want a new one. Let's not do something here that we'll regret."

They started to surround me.

"We won't regret this," one of the Royal Council said. "We'll enjoy this."

"Oh, yeah," I said, panic rising in my voice. "Won't you regret killing your king?" They kept coming. "You kill me and I can't do... you know... king stuff." I wasn't making a very convincing argument.

"You kill him," Gordy said, "and you'll never find the Source."

They stopped. Confusion clouded their purple faces.

I could kiss Gordy for coming to the rescue. Why I didn't think of it, I don't know. In my defense, it's not easy to think with a couple hundred Délons bearing down on you.

The general moved around the table. He motioned with his hand for the advancing Délons to go back outside. The Royal Council was still bristling. They wanted me dead, and I wasn't sure how long their need for the Source was going to keep them at bay. I could hear Canter laughing in my head. He was enjoying both the Délons' frustration and my terror. "Your friend uses his pretty tongue wisely," he thought.

"Not usually," I said out loud.

Reya leapt onto the table and dove on top of me. "Do not speak!" Her mandibles shot out of her mouth.

General Roy peeled her off me. Not to save me from her, but

to get me to himself. He lifted me by the throat. "A human shall never kill a shunter. It is law."

"The Source," I said through squeezed vocal cords.

He tossed me to the ground. "The law is clear. You must die."

"But it's also clear..." I could barely breathe let alone speak. "I'm the key to the Source."

He turned on Gordy. "A life for a life!"

"Stop!" I yelled. I stood with difficulty.

"Oz..." Gordy managed to say before the general's hand clamped down on his throat.

"Let him go!"

The general squeezed tighter and tighter. Gordy could not breathe. His face was turning blue. I rushed the general, but Reya grabbed me by the arm and tossed me aside.

Canter moved silently into my line of sight. "Tell him," he said without speaking, "The Pure lives."

I looked at Canter with a puzzled expression. He nodded his upside down head. "If you want to save your friend with the pretty tongue, tell him the Pure lives."

"The..." I started weakly. The strength had gone out of my voice. I sighed deeply and then shouted. "The Pure is alive!"

Every dead eye in the building focused on me. The general's grip on Gordy's throat loosened. His blue cheeks turned red.

"The Pure," a Royal Councilman said. He fell to his knees and appeared to be praying. "He's alive."

The general let go of Gordy and let him fall to the floor. He turned his sights on me. "What do you know of the Pure?"

I looked at Canter for guidance, but he turned and strolled away. "He's alive," I said.

"That's not possible," Reya said confused, "He is dead. We all saw him fall."

Délon City

I looked into the face of every Délon in the room. They were scared. Canter had given me a key piece of information. The Délons were terrified of this Pure guy and him being alive did not fit into their plans.

"What can I say?" I managed a wicked grin. "He got back up, and he ain't happy."

"You're lying," the General snapped. "The collective would know if the Pure lived."

"Well," I said, "I guess the collective is out of order because old Mr. Pure is alive and kicking, and you're on his 'get even' list. Understand?" I looked over at Gordy. He was massaging his throat and in obvious pain, but he was alive.

"How could you know this?" one of the Royal Council asked.

I scanned my brain for a feasible lie. "You think you're the only one who knows I'm the key to the Source. The Pure knows, and he's made a very generous offer."

"We're dead!" a member of the Royal Council screamed.

"Kill the human," another one shouted. "Better to never know the Source than to risk the Pure finding it first."

"Hold up," I said panic rising in my voice. "Let's not do anything hasty."

Reya turned to Roy. "The Royal Council is right. Kill the human. The Pure cannot find the Source."

It was apparent I had overplayed my hand. "Wait! Wait! Hear me out. I want what you want!" When those words came out of my mouth time stood sill. I saw Mrs. Dayton's scribbled handwriting on her notepad. "You want what they want."

"What is it we want?" the general asked setting time back in motion.

"Control," I said staring off into space. "The way it was before..." I focused on General Roy. "Before you killed the Pure, or thought you killed the Pure."

175

"It had to be done," the general said.

"Why?" I asked.

He ignored the question. "Miles will escort you to the incubation center." He walked away. As he passed by Miles, I heard him say, "He enters the center alone."

Pop, if it was possible to still call him that, grabbed my Mom by the arm and practically dragged her out of the lobby after General Roy.

The Royal Council turned their attention to the screamers in front of them. They continued to feed and only gave me passing glances as they gorged themselves.

Reya approached. "The general finds value in you."

"And you don't."

"I should do the collective a favor now and snap your neck."

I cleared my throat. "General Roy will kill you himself if you do."

"Then I die with honor."

I backed away. "You can kill me tomorrow. I've got things to do tonight." I moved to Gordy's side and helped him to his feet. "Get up to the room and keep an eye on Lou."

"Gee, I'm doing swell," he said sarcastically. "Thanks for asking."

"Don't let anybody..." I looked at Reya. "Or anything in. Okay?"

Still massaging his neck, he nodded. "I'm a fourteen-year-old kid outnumbered about a billion to one..." He shrugged his shoulders. "Don't worry. Nobody's getting past me." He looked at me smugly. "I'll just lock the door. That'll keep the bad guys out." He turned and headed for the elevator. "I liked it better when I used to tell you what to do."

"So did I," I said.

Délon City

***

As instructed, Miles escorted me to the incubation center. We didn't speak on the ride there. I couldn't help but think of Miles and Devlin as they used to be. Devlin was the fat kid who was always looking for that next chocolate bar, and Miles was his best friend and fellow troublemaker. They were two peas in a pod, as my grandmother used to say. Yet, now Devlin wasn't even a speck of a thought in Miles's Délon brain.

The incubation center was an old hangar at the airport, a large metal building with 100 foot ceilings. It was long enough for at least two football fields and wide enough to park two jumbo jets sideways. It was heavily guarded by Délons.

It took three Délons on each side to open the enormous doors. The smell of Délon City seemed to originate inside the hangar. I could almost see pillars of odor propping up the death dome overhead. Miles and I dismounted. I stood at the doorway looking into the cavernous hangar wondering if I had the courage to enter.

"Go," Miles barked. "I don't have all day."

"Got a full day of kissing the general's butt in front of ya', huh?"

He ignored my remark. "The general's stock is in the back. You'll know it when you see it."

"Why do you suppose he wanted me to go in alone?"

Miles shrugged his shoulders. "Don't know. Don't care." He started to walk away.

"C'mon, take a guess."

He stopped and peered over his shoulder at me. "He doesn't want you to come out alive."

I swallowed hard. "I guess taking a weapon with me is out of the question."

He walked over to Chubby and pulled J.J. off the saddle. "Take it," he said tossing it to me.

I was appreciative, but confused. "I thought it was against your law for a human to kill shunters."

"It is," he said. "But the shunters are the least of your problems in there."

I stared into the enormous dark building. The little light from outside seeped in, and I could make out piles of solifipods throughout the hangar. Some looked as high as mountains.

"You want to clue me in?" I asked Miles.

"No," he said.

"You don't want to give your king a fair shake? It would be nice to know what to look out for in there."

He climbed on his horse. "Look out for the Long Legs."

"Long legs?"

He steered his horse west. "No need for me to wait. If you make it out alive, you know the way back." With that he tapped his horse in the rib cage with his heel and rode off.

"Great," I mumbled under my breath. "Just great."

I breathed in deeply and blew out a long steady stream of air. A blip of a vision of Lou popped into my head, and I knew I didn't have a choice. I had to enter. I was inside the hangar before I had time to talk myself out of it. The Délons closed the door behind me.

The shunters must have sensed my presence because as I got closer to the first pile of solifipods they chirped in unison. It was a deafening clatter that hurt my eardrums. I put a finger in one ear and held the other ear to my shoulder while holding on to J.J.

I felt something move to my left. I turned, but it was too dark to see. I crept forward. There was a light coming from the back of the hangar so I followed it. Mountains of solifipods surrounded me. I was in a maze created in someone's sick

Délon City

nightmare. Something moved again, it zipped across one of the solifipod mounds. It was too fast for me to see, but I got the sense that it was very big. Some more movement to my right. I carried on. My empty backpack served as a constant reminder that I was on a life or death mission. I heard quick, scattered footsteps – dozens of them. Long Legs, I presumed.

The hangar was so big I almost felt like I needed a rest half way through it. My nerves were on end with the chirping shunters, the invisible Long Legs scurrying around me, and the pressure of finding the general's line before Lou's brain liquefied.

I stepped through a line of solifipod mounds and was forced to take a hard right when two huge solifipod hills blocked my way. A rope dangled in front of me. I knocked it to the side and passed. The rope was too stiff to swing. It moved to the side like a stiff tree branch, snapping back as soon as I let go of it. It brushed the top of my head as I passed, sending a chill down my spine. Another rope appeared, and then another. I looked up. A dark oval mass hovered above my head. I scanned the ropes and discovered they weren't ropes. They were legs, long legs. I was standing underneath a giant Daddy Long Legs spider. It must have been twenty feet tall. An enormous mouth on the underside of its body made a horrific sucking noise. I raced forward, swinging J.J. back and forth as I ran. The legs were long and luckily easy to cut through. The giant Long Legs toppled to the hangar floor. I stopped and turned to admire my work only to see every mound I had just passed covered in giant Long Legs, and all of them were fixated on me.

Part of me just wanted to give up, to lie down, and the let the Long Legs have me, but I knew it wasn't possible. Lou needed me. I raised J.J. in the air and ran through the solifipod maze. The Long Legs scurried after me. The sucking noise grew in volume the faster I ran. They were either really hungry or really mad, either way it didn't look good for me.

I rounded another line of solifipod mounds only to run into a wall of even bigger mounds. There was no way around. I had found my first dead-end in the maze, and it couldn't have come at a worse moment. I didn't have to turn around to know that an army of Long Legs was in hot pursuit. I had only one choice. I had to climb the solifipod mound in front of me. It nearly reached the ceiling.

Scaling a hundred-foot mountain of slimy pulsating solifipods is not the easiest thing to do. It was made even harder by the fact that I was being followed by twenty-foot spiders at a very fast pace. I just hoped that there weren't any Long Legs waiting for me at the top of the mound.

A Long Leg brushed my ankle. I reached down and swiped it with my sword and cut off a three foot section of one of its legs, but the spider kept moving forward on its seven remaining legs. Its Long Leg friends weren't far behind.

I was three quarters of the way up the mound when I decided there was no way I was going to make it. I wasn't going to let them eat me without a fight, but I knew there was no way I could win this. I closed my eyes and prayed. I wasn't even sure if God was in this twisted world, but I figured it couldn't hurt.

My sword in hand, I raised it above my head and prepared to bring it down on the first Long Legs that reached me, but to my surprise someone or something grabbed my wrist and dragged me up the mound. I saw a crab-like beast leap from the mound onto the nearest Long Leg... a silencer. I looked up at the person or thing that was dragging me and saw the upside down face of Canter peering down at me. To my left and to my right, other silencers leapt from the mound and attacked the advancing Long Legs.

Canter reached the top of the mound and pulled me to my

feet.

I looked at him, grateful but suspicious.

"A favor," he thought.

"What's the price?"

He looked confused. "Price?"

"What do I owe you in return?"

"You'll know soon enough." A Long Legs reached the top of the mound. "Find your new shunter and get out of here." With that, he rushed the giant spider. I watched as he started to tear it apart leg by leg. "Go!" He shouted in my head.

I jumped down the mound, lost my footing, and tumbled head over feet to the concrete floor of the hangar, banging my knee. I screamed in pain, but managed to stand. Somehow, J.J. was still in my hand. I limped toward the light in the back of the hangar. The mounds got progressively smaller the closer I got to the light. The sounds of the silencers ripping the Long Legs to shreds echoed throughout the metal building. I imagined the Long Legs were getting their licks in as well, but the silencers by their very nature did not scream or yell out in pain.

I reached the lighted area. It was an exit sign. My second dead-end. Miles said I would know the general's stock when I saw it, but he never said it would be easy to find. I yelled in frustration. My knee was killing me. I was covered in slime from the solifipods. Giant Daddy Long Legs chased me. I owed a tongue eating crab-man a favor for saving my life, and on top of it all, I could spend the next week inside the hangar and never find the general's precious solifipod stock. Lou deserved a better hero than me.

I sat down on the floor with my back against the door below the exit sign. I wanted to cry, but I was too tired. I closed my eyes, and tried to wish myself out of the hangar. The aches and pains my body had collected over the last couple of days pushed their way into my consciousness. I hurt all over. I grimaced, shifted, and squirmed, trying to find a comfortable position while I sat and contemplated how many ways I had failed. My mind was about to settle on my first misstep when I felt the ground shake. I opened my eyes. The ground shook again. I looked right, then left. Nothing. The ground shook again. I tried to stand, but my knee had stiffened. The pain was too intense. A little voice in my head was screaming for me to run. The ground shook again. This time it was followed by a high-pitched screech. I looked to my left again, and to my great disappointment, I finally saw what was causing the commotion, a Long Legs – the granddaddy of all the Long Legs. It must have been fifty feet high, and I got the sickening feeling it was looking for me. While it had no eyes that I could see, it still seemed to spot me. It let out a series of short screeches, almost like it was laughing maniacally. I tried to push myself up, but I couldn't. Fear had joined the pain in my body and completely immobilized me.

The Long Legs approached. Each step it took shook the entire hangar. I held on to J.J. feebly. I was dead. I had accepted that much, but that didn't mean I was happy about it. Maybe I could give the mutant spider one last jab before it sucked me into its ugly mouth.

When it reached me, it probed my face with one of its thin long legs. I knocked it away. It stooped and brought its massive oval shaped body down to my level. It did have eyes. Millions of tiny black eyes outlined its body. Two smaller legs that had been folded underneath its body, reached out for me. I flinched. The Long Legs screeched in disapproval. The smaller legs weren't legs at all. They were hollow tubes. The Long Legs ran the hollow tubes across my face. It was smelling me. I almost laughed. I'm not sure why. It wasn't funny at all. I was about to be eaten by an ugly giant Long Legs, and it was smelling me first. I wondered if

Délon City

I farted if it would leave me alone.

The Long Legs retracted its hollow tubes and folded them back under its body. "Did I pass the smell test," I laughed.

Its body began to shudder. Its mouth started to make the sucking noise the other Long Legs had made, and it opened and closed, slowly at first and then more rapidly as time went on. I saw a purple hump appear through the mouth opening, surrounded by a thin transparent membrane. The Long Legs shuddered even more. It was vomiting. Slowly the purple hump got bigger and bigger. It wasn't until it was almost all the way out that I realized what it was. It was throwing up a solifipod. The general's stock.

The Long Legs seemed exhausted after it dropped the solifipod on the floor in front of me. It stood to its full height and clumsily walked away, leaving me grateful that it had not eaten me, and grateful it had given me what I came for. I removed the backpack and stuffed the solifipod inside. Pushing back the aches and pains I had allowed to creep in earlier, I stood and threw open the exit door.

To my surprise, Miles was waiting for me on his horse. He was holding onto Chubby's reigns.

"What are you doing here?" I asked.

He smirked. "The man in the white coat wants to see you."

"What?"

In a blink of an eye, the blackened Délon night disappeared.

***

"Send me back!" I demand.

The man in the white coat ignores me. He writes in his notebook.

I stand. "Send me back, now!"

"We've done enough for today," he insists, still scribbling in

183

his notebook.

I feel like pouncing on him, but I know it will bring nothing but trouble. I sit back down and collect myself. Think! Think! I have to get back. Lou needs me.

The man in the white coat gets up and moves to his desk. He looks for something in a pile of papers. I can't for the life of me figure out why he thinks this is so unimportant. Lou is going to die if I don't get back.

"We can continue this next week..." he says still going through the papers on his desk.

"I can't wait until next week."

"Why is that, Oz?" He glances over at me.

"I have to get the solifipod back to the condo!" I'm trying not to raise my voice.

"There's no such thing as a solifipod or Lou for that matter. The sooner you realize that, the sooner you're on the road to recovery."

I'm growing increasingly angry, and the man in the white coat is aware of it. "You said if I found the Source it might help..."

"It's obvious you don't know what this Source is, Oz." He moves back toward the couch.

"I..." He's listening. I can get him to send me back. "I'll know it when we get to that part of the story."

He looks at me with a curious expression. "That's the first time you've called this a story. Does that mean you know this isn't real?"

Without thinking I say, "I'm beginning to feel that way." Was I?

He sits back down in his chair and gives me a hard look. He rubs his chin. "If I put you back under, you mustn't dawdle any longer than you have to. We must find this Source. Do you understand?"

Délon City

I nod. "I only have to help Lou and find Ajax. I'll find the Source then. I know it."

He thinks over my terms and then nods. "Lay down," he says. "We'll give this one last try."

***

Getting the solifipod to open was the tricky part. They came out when they came out. Supposedly there was no coaxing them out. Gordy and I noticed that whenever I was near, the shunter chirped like crazy. "Ain't that cute?" Gordy smiled. "It likes you."

"Great," I said. "But it still won't open for me." We knelt (me on a very sore knee) around the coffee table trying to solve the puzzle of the reluctant shunter.

Lou was lying on the nearby sofa. She was running a fever, but she was still conscious. She kept a weary eye on us. Getting the solifipod to open was going to be the easy part compared to what she would have to do.

"Go get a knife out of the kitchen," I said.

"You're going to cut it open?"

"You got any other ideas?"

Gordy stood. "What about them?" He pointed out our penthouse window to the crawling Délons. "They ain't going to be too happy if you slice this puppy up."

I watched as the thick layer of Délons climbed all over each other. "Desperate times call for desperate measures. We'll deal with that when the time comes."

"You'll deal with it," he said walking toward the kitchen. "If they ask, I didn't know nothing about it."

He was in the kitchen for less than a minute. He emerged with a large knife with a black handle that had three brass rivets.

"I think it's one of them Ginsu knives. It can cut through a

185

metal pipe," he said proudly. "That's what they say on the infomercial anyway."

He handed it to me handle side out. I took it and placed the sharp side of the blade gently on top of the solifipod. Gordy positioned himself between the window and me. I shut my eyes and said a quick prayer. Opening my eyes, I bore down on the handle and began sawing the top of the solifipod. The solifipod hide was tough. The sharp knife didn't leave so much as a scratch. I bore down harder. Still nothing. I tightened my grip on the solifipod with my other hand. I stood trying to put my legs into it. My knife holding hand slipped and I stuck myself with the knife. I raised up, gritted my teeth, and sucked in air.

"Ahhhh," I said. "Damn!" I bled from a surface wound. The solifipod must have dulled the knife otherwise it would have cut my hand off. Drops of blood dripped down on the solifipod. The shunter began to chirp wildly. Gordy and I exchanged a glance. Seconds later, a small opening appeared on top of the solifipod.

"Dude," Gordy said, "the blood."

I held my bleeding hand over the solifipod and let the blood fall freely. The solifipod opened wider and wider. "Get Lou over here," I said.

Gordy was stunned by the sight of the solifipod opening. He snapped out of his brief trance and helped Lou off the couch.

Lou's eyes were slits. Her cheeks were beet red from fever. The rest of her complexion was ghost white. Her bloodshot eyes focused on the gaping opening in the solifipod.

"You know what you have to do, right?" I asked.

She nodded weakly.

"Do you want me to help?"

She shook her head, and I felt relieved.

She fell to her knees in front of the coffee table. She was

covered in sweat. She slowly lifted her right hand, still a little swollen from the previous sting, and let it hover over the opening in the solifipod.

She looked at me for reassurance. I smiled and tried to give her strength with a quick affirmative nod. I was scared to death for her, but I couldn't let her know it. She closed her eyes and shoved her hand in the opening.

Maybe two seconds passed before she screamed at such a pitch it seemed to vibrate every glass in the condo. The crawling Délons stopped in their tracks and turned their full attention to what we were doing. I pulled Lou up by her shoulders before the purple, dead-eyed freaks could see. The solifipod closed quickly. I was sure that none of the spies outside the window saw a thing.

I sat Lou down on the couch. Her regular color flew back into her face, and her eyes gradually opened wider and wider. She was slowly returning to the Lou I knew and loved. I sat down next to her.

She examined my face closely. "Don't be scared." With that she closed her eyes and rested her head on my shoulder. It was the first time since I found out the Délons were in charge that I was actually glad to be where I was. I felt like I was where I was supposed to be. I can't explain it. I just knew that being with Lou was where I was supposed to be.

SIXTEEN

We all slept until the next afternoon or at least what we thought was afternoon. There seemed to be only two times of day in Délon City, dark and slightly less dark. I realized after finding some peanut butter and crackers in the pantry that I hadn't formulated a plan to spring Ajax. I had been so consumed with worry for Lou that I had not given my old gorilla friend much thought beyond the conversation at dinner. He was part of the one-on-one match today, and I spent much of the afternoon trying to figure out ways of getting him out of that. But in the end I decided he's not the one you would have to worry about in a one-on-one match. It was the other poor sap that they had him matched up against that would have to worry. Ajax was the greatest warrior I had ever seen. I couldn't think of man, monster, or animal that was any match for him.

Lou, Gordy, and I engaged in very little conversation that day. Lou's hand was red from the two shunter stings, but the swelling had gone down. The welt on her face had become a very fine, almost indiscernible scratch. She had slept on my shoulder all night. When we woke up, we were both a little embarrassed. She wiped the spittle from her mouth and quickly pushed away from me. I stood with my eyes downcast and moved to the kitchen. It was weird, but in a good kind of way. It's really hard to explain.

Gordy was the first to notice that the crawling Délons were

Délon City

gone. He walked to the window as if it were it a huge gaping hole and he would be sucked out into the darkened sky at any moment. "What gives?" he asked.

Lou and I joined him. "They're gone," Lou said stating the obvious as some people do.

I looked down on the street below us. It was empty. "It's a ghost town..."

We all nearly jumped out of our skins when we heard a loud knock at the door. Lou covered her mouth with her hand holding back nervous laughter. Gordy's lips were pressed together. He stumbled back clamping his hand to his chest. His trademark. Faking a heart attack. I hadn't seen him do that... in a long time. It was strangely comforting.

I shook off the initial shock, and went to the door. "Yeah," I said. My mother would have killed me for such a rude greeting.

"Open up," the voice barked back.

I opened the door a crack and saw Délon Miles staring back at me.

"I am to escort you to the stadium." He pushed his way into the condo. "We must go now."

"What happened to everybody?" Gordy asked. He pointed to the window.

"They're at the stadium," Miles said.

Gordy squinted his eyes and tilted his head. "All of them?"

"It's a big day. Now, c'mon, let's go."

I grabbed my backpack with my new solifipod and waited as Lou and Gordy passed through the front door. Miles directed me to walk ahead of him, and we all moved to the elevator.

"What's so big about today?" Gordy asked.

Miles almost smiled. "One of our champions will die today."

"And that's a good thing?" Lou asked.

Miles looked at her perplexed. "It is a great thing."

R.W. Ridley

The elevator doors opened, and we all stepped inside. I was never more frightened for Ajax. I had confidence he would prevail, but at what price.

***

We arrived at what used to be the Georgia Dome. It was covered in a layer of Délons twenty feet thick. Literally, all the Délons in the city were here. This was bigger than the Super Bowl.

An opening in the massive Délon bubble formed to let Miles, Gordy, Lou, and me enter. I wasn't sure I really wanted to go inside. The deeper I got into the thick blanket of Délons, the more claustrophobic I felt. It was like we were voluntarily walking into the belly of the beast.

The hairs on the back my neck stood up. I got the sudden feeling that I was being watched, not just by the throngs of Délons all around me. Somebody else was watching me. I shook it off and returned my attention to the ghoulish scene around me.

Once inside the dome, we were escorted to the artificial turf. The seats, walls, and ceilings were crawling with Délons almost as thick as what was crawling outside. The dome looked like it was breathing with all the movement.

Only about twenty square yards of the field was left bare. I assumed this is where the one-on-one match would take place. The general stood in the middle of the clearing. I recognized the Falcons logo beneath his feet. He smiled his gut wrenching Délon smile when he saw us approach.

"Ah, our honored guests!" He met us and pulled me to the center of the logo. "Our king!" He shouted. Every Délon in the building erupted in cheers. The sound was deafening and painful.

"Today," he continued, "one champion will die for our king!"

Délon City

The Délons exploded again, louder than before. "And another champion will kill for our king!" The noise level shook the ground beneath us. It felt as though the very structure of the Georgia Dome would crumble, but it held up. I looked at Lou and Gordy. They were as scared as I was. There was a bloodlust in the air that nearly smothered us. I tried to fake a smile to reassure them, but they knew a fake when they saw one.

The crowd to the right of us parted. Four Délons pulling chains entered the dome through a tunnel. At the end of the chains, Ajax struggled to break free. My heart dropped when I saw him. His face was scarred and he looked twice his normal size. One of his eyes was swollen shut. He had been marked. Recently. I knew it. I could smell it. Not just once. Many times. This is how they prepared their champions to fight.

I almost cried because I knew the hatred and pain that was running through Ajax's veins. He wanted to kill. More than that, he needed to kill.

The crowd to the left of us parted. The other champion was about to emerge. First out of the tunnel was a man I recognized. Hollis. Pepper Sands's right-hand man. He was the one who told us about HMI, Hyper Mental Imaging. He was Pepper's team psychologist when Pepper was smashing heads as the Falcon's leading tackler. What was he doing here?

The answer to my question came almost as the thought left my head. Following close behind him was Pepper. The other champion.

Lou turned to me when she recognized him. Her eyes said everything. Don't let this happen.

I nodded. I don't know why because I was pretty sure there was nothing I could do. The Délons came to see a murder today, and one way or another they were going to see it.

By the look of Pepper's swollen eye, it was clear he had been marked for this fight as well. The Délons dressed him in pair of cutoff sweat pants. His muscles were inflated by the marking, but it appeared he was still about 300 pounds lighter than Ajax. He didn't stand a chance.

The champions reached the fringe of the clearing. The general raised his hand to silence the crowd. Remarkably, almost instantaneously, the Délons fell silent. If it wasn't for the gargled grunts of Ajax, you could have heard a pin drop.

"Today, we have yet another treat!" General Roy shouted. The crowd of Délons in front of us parted. Standing on what was once the visitor's sidelines were two Délons propping up Newell by his arms. "Today, we have captured our Keeper!"

Once again, the Délons erupted.

I swallowed. Wes and the others?

The general, as if he read my mind, pointed to the still parting crowd. I watched in horror as the Délons peeled back and revealed Wes holding Valerie. Tyrone stood beside him holding onto the scruff of Kimball's neck. Reya stood by them like a hunter standing by a fresh kill.

"Friends of yours?" The general asked.

I didn't answer him. He knew. He'd known all along.

"This isn't a game, Oz," he said in a low steady tone. "You can't escape the collective."

"What are you going to do to them?"

"The same thing I did to him," The general said motioning to the crowd behind me. I turned to see Miles dragging a body out of the crowd. Devlin. Dead. Beaten horribly. Tortured to death.

I surveyed the scene. Ajax and Pepper were mad with hate. Lou and Gordy were panic-stricken. Wes, Valerie, and Tyrone were scared but stoic. And Kimball was ready to do battle. I smiled.

Délon City

"What are you smiling at?" The general asked.

"You made a mistake," I said.

His spider legs began to dance. He didn't like my demeanor. "Mistake?"

I focused on his dead eyes to convey to him that I meant every word of what I was about to say. "You brought me my warriors."

He smashed me in the face with the back of his fist and sent me crashing to the artificial turf. Kimball tore free from Tyrone's grip and bolted to my defense. He was too quick for the Délons to catch. My faithful dog leapt through the air and clamped his teeth around the general's neck.

I was too stunned by the general's blow to react immediately. I lay on my back and watched the dome spin. I heard the general cry out, followed by Kimball yelping in pain.

"No!" I screamed, my jaw throbbing. Kimball's lifeless body fell next to me. The general had broken his neck. The anger and coldness I had experienced after my marking came back. Tears stung my eyes. The hate that haunted and tortured me that night re-emerged. I slammed my fist into the artificial turf and was only mildly surprised when I created a hole in the seemingly impenetrable surface.

I jumped to my feet and rushed the general. I had the strength of ten men and I was going to use it to tear him apart. I threw my shoulder into his abdomen and we both tumbled to the stadium floor. I pounded my fists into General Roy's purple face before he could gain any sense of understanding what was happening to him.

Chaos broke out around us, but none of the Délons ran to the general's aid. Ajax broke free from his chains and was crushing Délons like they were brittle twigs. They had juiced him beyond their control. They created a champion that could easily dispose of them by the dozens.

Pepper was never one to stand on the sidelines. He dove into the crowd of Délons next to him and used the hate that they built up inside of him against them. He wasn't as proficient as Ajax at killing Délons, but he was taking them down two at a time.

Newell took the opportunity created by the distraction to break free from the two Délons who had a hold of him. He shed his robe. A light emanated from him that at once held everyone's attention in the stadium. As quickly as the melee had begun, it stopped. My fist halted mid-punch. I couldn't move. The noise was vacuumed out of the air. Silence.

Newell walked toward me. Every Délon, animal, and human was frozen in time. I was the only who could move besides Newell. I stood, searching for the hate I was filled with just seconds before.

"What," I began.

"Do you know where you are?" Newell asked bending down to stroke Kimball's head.

What an odd question. I looked around the dome. One-by-one I saw Délon after Délon pop like a balloon. They were disappearing. "What's happening?"

"I asked you a question," he said still attending to Kimball. "Do you know where you are?"

"I'm... in Délon City..."

Newell patted Kimball and the dog's tail began to wag.

"Kimball!" I ran to his side. "He's alive."

"More like his death has been erased," Newell said.

Kimball stood and shook like he'd just had a bath. I hugged him hard enough for him to whine and pull away.

"You're in a story, Oz," Newell said. "A story in which you don't belong."

"Don't belong?" The crowd of Délons rapidly grew smaller

Délon City

and smaller. "That's the second time you've told me I don't belong. If I don't belong, how did I get here?"

He leaned in and whispered, "You're on a couch in Dr. Graham's office."

I swallowed hard. "Dr. Graham..."

"He has you under hypnosis."

"Don't trust 'G.'"

"He's not who you think he is."

My head started spinning. This was all too insane for me to comprehend. "What do I do?"

"Don't lead him to the Source."

"That's easy. I don't know what it is. I don't want to know."

"You will before this day is over."

"I'm confused."

"It's about to get a whole lot more confusing." He gestured for me to look to my right. I was looking at the Georgia Dome from outside.

"How..." I looked down. I was still standing on the artificial turf.

"You will begin again."

"Begin what?"

"You are entering the dome again."

I watched as Lou, Gordy, Miles and I began making our way through the Délon opening into the stadium.

"Let them fight. No matter what happens, let them fight."

"Ajax and Pepper?"

"It has a place in this story. It must happen."

"Ajax will kill Pepper."

"And in doing so, he will ensure that the future of the Storytellers is secure."

"I can't let Pepper die."

"If you don't, then you leave the fate of the Storytellers in the hands of the Destroyers."

I couldn't believe my ears. "Pepper would never betray the Storytellers."

"Not intentionally, no." Newell started to back away. "I've given you a second chance to do nothing. I'm pleading with you to let them fight. Let Pepper die." He took one more step and disappeared, and I was no longer standing on the artificial turf. I was entering the dome as I had done moments before. The events of the past few minutes began to scramble in my brain. I watched them like a movie in my mind's eye, only segments were thrown together out of sequence.

"Are you all right?" Lou asked.

I gave her an unenthusiastic nod and smile. She didn't know. This was all happening for the first time for her. I was the only one who remembered.

We entered the clearing where General Roy was waiting for us. The Délons were back in full force, crawling, waiting for the fight to begin.

"Ah, our honored quests!" The general began. He attempted to pull me to the center of the Falcons logo as he had done before, but I broke from his slimy grip and continued on through the horde of Délons.

"Where are you going?" The general asked.

"To talk to my champion," I said.

He stood, embarrassed that I had usurped his authority. He could have insisted that I return, signaled to the Délons to prevent me from passing through, but he didn't. He went on with his speech about one champion who would die for his king and one who would kill for his king.

I made it to the tunnel entrance where Ajax had emerged before. The four Délons stood at the mouth of the tunnel holding onto the chains with all their might. They were being tugged to and fro.

I walked past them and stood face-to-face with Ajax. He had dwarfed me before, but now, he was twice as big. He huffed and grunted and dug at the thick metal collar around his neck. He was too agitated to take notice of me yet. His face was deeply scarred. The wisdom that used to dwell in his penetrating stare was gone. The swollen eye was as big as a grapefruit, but the other eye was fierce and beyond angry. He rose up and pounded his chest, pock-pock-pock. That's when he noticed me. He stopped as if on command.

"Ajax," I said. "It's me."

He blew air through his massive nostrils, and let out a vocalization that emanated from his throat.

"It's Oz." I said.

He lurched forward. The Délons pulled back on the chains. Ajax stumbled.

It pained me to see him in such a state. He was being tortured by the thoughts that were soaring through his marked brain. He wasn't the Ajax I knew and loved. Then again, I wasn't sure if I was the same Oz. I stepped forward, and he seemed to be startled by my lack of fear. The truth is I was scared to death. I wasn't even sure what I was doing. I felt compelled to ease his anguish. He was my friend, and he was going to kill Pepper. I knew that it was against his nature to kill humans. The marking would wear off, and when it did, he would be stuck with the memory of what he'd done. I'm not sure he would be able to live with himself. He had been raised by a human, taught to speak American Sign Language. He was a gentle being at heart.

I hooked my bent right index finger, palm facing down, over the bent left index finger, palm facing up, and then reversed the position of the hands and repeated the gesture.

Ajax snorted and shook his head.

I signed the word for "friend" again.

Ajax snarled his lip and planted his knuckles on the concrete floor of the tunnel. The four Délons holding his chains watched with mild interest as their champion calmed.

I made the sign again.

Ajax sat on his haunches and raised his massive arms. He made an 'L' shape with his right hand and touched the right side of his forehead. Palm facing left, he moved the right hand downward, landing across the thumb side of the left 'L' hand, palm facing right.

I didn't understand the sign. He repeated it. I shrugged my shoulders. He shook his head and grunted, clearly frustrated. If I had to guess, he was calling me a loser.

My sign language vocabulary was limited. I pulled out the ones I could remember. I turned up my left palm and made two quick brushing movements with the fingertips of my right hand. "Forgive." I pointed to him.

He cocked his head to the right. He was mulling over my sign. What was I forgiving him for? I bowed my head. If he only knew.

The crowd of Délons parted, making way for his entrance. I smiled and nodded before I bolted through the cleared pathway back toward the general and the others.

General Roy watched me approach with a confused look on his face. He wanted to know what I had been up to. I ran up to him.

"Save the dramatics," I said. "I know everything."

"Everything?" He squinted his dead eyes.

"Pepper Sands is Ajax's opponent." I pointed to the tunnel where Pepper would soon emerge. "Newell is behind that crowd of freaks." I pointed to the Délons standing in front of us. "And a little farther to the right are my friends. Like I said, I know

Délon City

everything."

He was angry that I had ruined his surprise. He wanted to ask how, but he didn't want to give me the satisfaction. So I offered up a lie to get under his skin a little deeper.

"The Pure knows all."

He shook with anger.

Having sufficiently pissed him off, I quickly moved to the other tunnel. I fought my way through the Délons to the tunnel opening. This was going to be harder. I had to say goodbye to a dead man.

Hollis greeted me with a startled expression as he saw me approach. "Oz?"

"Dr. Hollis."

He smiled. "Well, I'll be. It is you." He stepped toward me, not knowing whether a hug or handshake was appropriate. At the last second, he opted for the handshake. I grabbed his hand and shook it firmly. "How about that? You're about an inch taller, but it's you all right. Hey, Pep, look who it is."

The beefed up Pepper stepped out of the shadows. He peered at me with his open eye. The veins on his forehead were throbbing. His lips had a blue tint. He was shivering. He was freezing inside. It was painfully obvious.

"Pepper," I said.

He nodded his head. I'm not sure he recognized me.

"It's Oz, Pepper," Hollis said. He turned to me. "He's not really himself right now. They..."

"Marked him," I said pointing to my once swollen eye.

Hollis's shoulders dropped. He knew what my marking meant. I was to become a Délon. "They do it before every match. He's a crowd favorite."

"And you?" I asked. "What's your function here?" It came off as accusatory when I didn't mean it to be.

R.W. Ridley

"I'm his handler. Pepper worked out a deal with the Délons. He'll be their champion as long as I'm spared," he pointed to my eye. "You know."

"Yeah," I said.

Pepper stared at me.

"October 2004," I said. "Against Tampa Bay, you had two sacks, a fumble recovery, and an interception return for a touchdown. You were a one man wrecking crew."

He managed a smile. "Still am, kid. I still am."

"Show me a hero and I will write you a tragedy," I said.

It was Pepper's turn to cock his head in confusion.

"You told me that once," I said.

"F. Scott Fitzgerald," he said.

I nodded.

"Today's not my day for a tragedy, kid."

I smiled feebly. "You're Pepper Sands!"

"I'm Pepper Sands!" He barked back. He pounded his chest with his fists.

I wanted to tell him to turn and run, to get the hell out of the stadium, Délon City, the United States, hell, to get off the damn planet, but I couldn't. His fate was sealed, and there was nothing I could do about it.

***

General Roy had prodded me to join him in the luxury box before the match officially got underway, but I rejected his offer for many reasons. Not the least of which was that my parents, or what used to be my parents, were waiting for me up there. I couldn't stand to see them again. It would have been yet another reminder of how badly I had failed.

After Devlin was revealed to me this time, Newell was dragged

200

Délon City

out in front of the Délons, and beaten severely. The crowd cheered uproariously with each blow he received from his two Délon escorts. It was sickening. I knew that Newell had the power to stop it, just as he had done before, but he didn't. He took the beating because it was part of the story. He was willing to die if meant ending the coming of all seven races of Destroyers. I got a lump in my throat as I realized for the first time what a real hero was.

The general allowed Wes, Valerie, Tyrone, and Kimball to stay with me on the edge of the clearing. I'm not sure why exactly. Part of me thought he was a little afraid of me now that he thought I was in communication with the Pure. But only a little. He was beginning to believe as Reya did, that it would be safer to kill me so that the Pure couldn't use me to find the Source.

Before the fight began I turned to Lou. "Do you remember any of Ajax's sign language?"

"Some," she said.

"What about this?" I repeated the sign Ajax had given me in the tunnel.

She thought it over, repeating it several times herself. "Oh," she yelped as it came to her. "Brother."

I stared at her in disbelief. "Brother?" I whispered.

"Why?" she asked.

I didn't answer. Did Ajax consider me a brother? What was he telling me?

The Délons still had Ajax on his chains. He was more agitated than he had been before. He was ready for a fight.

Pepper stood stoically. Hollis was saying something to him. Trying to get him to visualize every aspect of the fight, I imagined. Trying to predetermine Pepper's victory. It wouldn't come.

Lou saw me staring at Pepper. "How are we going to stop this?"

I didn't acknowledge her.

"Oz, how..."

"We're not!" I barked.

She was hurt by both my tone and my answer. "What do you mean?"

"Just what I said."

"But Ajax will kill him."

I thought of Newell taking the beating when he didn't have to. I thought of a thousand other sacrifices that I had heard about in my lifetime. They all were about men and women sacrificing themselves for the greater good. I couldn't recall one story where someone let their friend die for the greater good. It was a far greater sacrifice.

"Oz," Lou continued.

"What can I do?"

"What..." She bit her lip. "Don't you remember the comic book? Stevie made you a hero."

"That was a different time and a different story. I'm not the hero here."

As the words left my mouth, the four Délons holding onto Ajax's chains let go. He immediately leapt on one of them and broke its neck in the blink of an eye. He turned his fury on the crowd of Délons behind him.

"Hey!" A shout came from the other end of the clearing. Pepper stepped forward.

Ajax turned toward him. Rage and fury rose from him like heat waves from a searing blacktop. I felt the feeling rise in me as well. Again, I was able to call up the rage and strength I had endured and demonstrated immediately after my marking. I fought it. It would drive me to interfere, and I knew I couldn't.

"You big dumb ape," Pepper shouted. "The fight's over here!"

Ajax spun around and let out a tongueless roar that sounded like a lion with a gag over its mouth.

Délon City

Lou grabbed my arm. She was looking to me for strength when all I wanted to do was turn and run like hell.

"Lord help me," Wes said. "This ain't a fight. It's an execution." He was still holding Valerie in his arms and, at that moment, she buried her tear-stained face into his shoulder.

"Ajax won't kill him," Tyrone said. "He's a good guy."

I envied his hope and innocence. I wanted to believe in the good in Ajax desperately. But I knew now that good warriors are forced to do bad things in the name of the mission. The mission here was to save the world from the Destroyers and bring everything back to the way it was. Pepper's death would bring us closer to that.

Pepper rushed Ajax and grabbed one of his chains. He tried to pull him to the center of the clearing, but Ajax pulled back on the chain and sent Pepper flying into the crowd of Délons to the side. Ajax leapt into the crowd after him and they both momentarily disappeared into the swarm. It wasn't long until Délons were flying everywhere, discarded like the trash they were.

Ajax and Pepper tumbled out of the Délon horde. Their arms were locked. Ajax could have easily snapped Pepper's arm in half, but he didn't. In fact, Pepper tossed Ajax back into the wall of Délons, and in doing so took out more of the purple pukes. This was the theme of the match, both fighters would manage to toss the other into the Délons, and squash as many in the crowd as they could. This went on for what seemed hours, but in reality was ten minutes tops.

I glanced at the luxury boxes and could see the displeasure on the general's face. Délons were not to suffer at the hands of their champions, yet here they were falling like pins in a bowling alley. And nothing could be done because it was collateral damage.

Hollis stepped out and with both palms facing up, and both hands bent, he brought them downward on each side of his body.

Lou and I both saw him at the same time. She spoke the sign out loud "Now!"

The fighters didn't see him immediately. They continued to pummel each other to force one another into the Délons. It was Pepper who spotted him first. He freed himself from Ajax and bolted for the middle of the clearing. Ajax didn't follow. He jumped to the edge of the clearing, and shook his head violently. Why didn't he follow his opponent? He let out a pained cry.

Pepper stood and faced him. He was bruised and battered. His chest was rising and falling rapidly as he fought to catch his breath. He himself gave Ajax the "Now" sign.

Ajax stood on two legs and pounded his chest. He shook his head again. Pepper repeated the sign. The crowd began to stomp and sway. They were growing impatient.

Hollis fell to the turf in tears. What was going on? It was as if Pepper was giving up. More than that, it was as if... he, Hollis, and Ajax had planned it.

Ajax slowly, hesitantly made his way to the center of the clearing. The Délons were growing more and more impatient. They sensed a kill, and they were screaming for blood.

I watched slack jawed as Pepper gave the sign for "Brother."

With one horrifying blow with the back of his massive hand, Ajax sent Pepper flying backwards and tumbling to the turf. Ajax had done what he was supposed to do. He killed his brother and fellow warrior.

SEVENTEEN

The man in the white coat does not know how to react. I brought myself out of hypnosis. I had watched Pepper die, and he would not be the last. I didn't want to be in the story any more. I didn't have the heart for it.

He scribbles something on a piece of paper. "Chester is on his way. He and I will escort you to your room. We'll stop along the way at the pharmacy. I have a new prescription I want you to try."

"Drugs?"

He raises an eyebrow as he peers up from his clipboard. "Medication. To make you better."

"Why do you use that word?"

"What word?"

"Better. Better than what?"

He smirks. "What a strange question. You're sick, Oz. I'm trying to make you better."

"You're not really."

"Of course I am." He becomes uneasy. "Why else do you think you're here?"

I sit up. "You want to know the Source."

Chester enters the office. "You rang, Doc."

The man in the white coat keeps his eyes on me. "Mr. Griffin will be going back to his room." He stands, and I notice his hands are shaking. "I'll be coming with you. We need to stop at the pharmacy along the way."

Chester approaches me. "With or without restraints, Doc?"

"Dr. Graham," I say.

"Yes," He says as he turns to me.

"Nothing," I reply. "I just wanted to say your name out loud."

"No restraints," Dr. Graham says to Chester.

"You sure? The pharmacy is down by..." He looks at me and then back at the doctor. "You know."

"It will be fine."

Chester puts a hand under my arm and helps me to my feet. He is a huge man. He was hired for his size not his brains. I had heard him say so on many occasions, although I'm not sure where or when. I'm not sure of anything.

We exit the office. Chester walks on my left still holding onto my arm. Dr. Graham walks on my right. There is something about their walks that catches my attention. It's so uniform. They have almost identical walks. I find this odd, although I'm not sure why.

There are lines painted on the floor, a yellow line, a green line, and a red line. The sign above us breaks the building into sections. Yellow is pharmacy, women's dorms, and examination rooms. Green is detention ward, treatment room A, and group room. Red is cafeteria, recreation room, treatment room B, and men's dorm. We follow the yellow line.

As we pass people in the hall, I can't help but recognize their faces. I don't know how I know them, but I do. Some look at me with an angry glare, others an encouraging smile.

I am struck with the feeling that none of us belong here. My problem is that I don't know if my feelings can be trusted. Maybe I do belong here, and I'm just looking for a way out.

Dr. Graham is in front of me. I watch the back of his head

as he leads us toward the pharmacy. I wait for the first spider leg to pop out. He is a Délon. He has to be. Don't trust 'G.'

I pass a woman standing in the doorway. She is old, too old to be alive by the looks of her. She raises her right arm. Her hand is missing.

At the pharmacy, I wait with Chester while Dr. Graham enters the small room. The people passing us in the hallway look like the living dead. They walk, heads down, shuffling their feet.

Two orderlies approach pushing a gurney, a body under a sheet. Chester forgets about me and joins his coworkers.

"Who kicked it?"

"Sands," the younger of the two orderlies replies.

"He had some help," the older orderly replies.

"What do you mean?" Chester asks.

"They found the new patient from 22A in his room."

"The deaf mute – big hairy guy?"

"Yeah, man," the younger orderly replies. "He was huddled in the corner grunting like a gorilla."

"No way! I always miss the fun," Chester laments.

I listen to their conversation in disbelief. At one point, I cover my ears. They aren't real. None of this is real. I have to keep telling myself this place isn't real.

I open the pharmacy door and step inside unnoticed. Dr. Graham is behind the counter talking with the pharmacist. Their conversation is casual. I can tell they are old friends.

"So, this is for the DH perp?" The pharmacist says.

"He's not a perp, Bill. He's a patient."

"He killed two people, Doc. He's dangerous."

"All of our patients are dangerous," Dr. Graham says as he scans the shelves.

"Yeah, but most of them can be managed," he says as he shakes a bottle of pills to emphasize his point.

"Mr. Griffin can be, too," Graham replies. "We just haven't found the right cocktail."

"Chester says he thinks he's twelve, and he has no idea what he's done."

Dr. Graham looks angry. "Chester talks too much, and he thinks he's fourteen."

The pharmacist snickers. "He has no idea that he killed his wife and best friend?"

I swallow hard. My wife and best friend? My memory conjures up the time jump. I was standing over Lou with J.J. in my hand, and Canter had Gordy pinned against the wall.

"It's a traumatic event in his life. It's not unusual for a person to block memories he can't bear to relive over and over again." Dr. Graham joins the pharmacist and places three white bottles on the counter. "We're close to a breakthrough. He's looking for something he calls the Source when I have him under. I really think he wants to remember. Something in me believes he wants to get better."

I start to go cold. I don't want to hear what they are saying. I am Oz Griffin. I live on 334 Terrace Street in Tullahoma. I am 14 years old.

I close my eyes tight. I am not what they think. I open my eyes and watch from my darkened corner of the room as the pharmacist dumps the pills on a tray. He divides them into two groups with a straight-edged plastic tool.

Dr. Graham reaches for the second bottle and reads the label. For the first time, I notice his black fingernails, and the purple rash on his hand.

I can't take it anymore. I move quietly to the pharmacy door and exit. Chester is still chatting up his friends. They are practically giddy about the murder. They have forgotten I even exist.

Délon City

I follow the yellow line to a long corridor with a half dozen doors on either side. Flickering fluorescent lights hum above my head as I tiptoe down the hallway. I can see my distorted reflection in the laminate flooring. I am not the man staring back at me. I can't be.

A familiar sound comes from the door to my left. It's a high-pitched sucking noise. There is a porthole window in the door. I slide my feet closer and press my forehead against the glass. A young boy lies on a metal table in the middle of an otherwise empty room. There is something on his face.

I push the door open and step inside. I am strangely detached from where I am and what I am doing. It's as if I'm not here.

I reach the boy on the table, and I am not surprised at all to see a shunter attached to his face. The jellyfish blob seemingly screams with delight now that it has an audience. I look through the purple transparent flesh and see my eyes staring back at me. I am the boy on the table. I am the boy whose humanity is being sucked from his body. I stumble away from the table. There is a tightness in my chest that smothers me. I breathe in thick uneven waves.

"What is real?" A voice whispers in my head. Canter steps out of the darkest corner of the room.

"What's happening? I don't understand."

"Time is a funny thing when it doesn't matter any more. It comes and goes as it pleases." He strolls around the table. "You can be in two places at once." He gently strokes the shunter with one of his spiked fingers. "Three even."

The dark corner of the room lights up and reveals a large warehouse. I see myself again. I am pulling J.J. from Lou's stomach. Gordy is screaming bloody murder from the far end of the warehouse as Canter is mutilating him.

"Stop it! I don't want to see anymore."

"What are you feeling?" Canter asks.

I think about his question. I look down at myself on the table. The shunter is sucking with a grotesque fury. "Ashamed," I say.

I feel Canter smile. "He likes that answer."

"Who?"

"He would have accepted humbled, but ashamed is so much better." Canter moves away from the table. The warehouse gives way to the darkness.

"Who is he?"

Canter glides effortlessly toward the harsh shadows. "He is why you are here."

"What…"

"Did you really think you could drive a retarded boy to suicide and survive the guilt?"

The room begins to morph before my eyes. I slowly fade away from the table. The table shifts to an iron cot bolted to a padded wall. The room shrinks to a quarter its original size. My ankle is shackled to a bolt in the middle of the room.

"You're crazy, Oz Griffin. That's all you are."

I fall on the spongy mattress. The room is a bright haze of white. I am haunted once again by the flickering, humming fluorescent light above my head.

I chuckle. I'm crazy. That's all I am.

The End
Of
Book Two

210

538188

Made in the USA